GRIZZL

'CAUTIONARY TALES F͟O͟ ͟ ͟ ͟ ͟ ͟ ͟ QUEAM

D1100867

TERROR TIME TOYS

WARNING!

THIS BOOK IS **NOT** A TOY.
DO NOT LEAVE SMALL CHILDREN
ALONE WITH THIS BOOK OR THEY
MIGHT DIE OF FRIGHT!

YOU'RE NOT A GROWN UP. WHERE DO YOU THINK YOU'RE GOING?

Also in this series:

GRIZZLY TALES

'CAUTIONARY TALES FOR LOVERS OF SQUEAM'

TERROR TIME TOYS

JAMIE RIX

Illustrated by Steven Pattison

WARNING

THESE TALES CONTAIN SMALL LIES WHICH MAY BE HARMFUL IF SWALLOWED.

Orion
Children's Books

COME AWAY FROM THAT DOOR. THE HANDLE IS WIRED UP TO 10,000 VOLTS. YOU'LL FRY IF YOU TOUCH IT!*

For Charlotte and Jolyon

First published in Great Britain in 2008
by Orion Children's Books
a division of the Orion Publishing Group Ltd
Orion House
5 Upper St Martin's Lane
London WC2H 9EA
An Hachette Livre company

A catalogue record for this book is available from the British Library.

Printed in Great Britain

INSTRUCTIONS FOR
TERROR-TIME TOYS SURVIVAL

Now that you are stupid enough to be on the wrong side of the door, follow these instructions on how to survive the Terror Toys as if your life depended on it . . . which, as it happens, it does.

Empty your toy box and protect yourself with a plastic sword, a light sabre, a cap gun, and a bow and arrows (with red suckered tips).

Wear a sheriff's badge at all times. If you should be approached by hothell security and asked to present your room key, use traditional cop-speak such as, 'Freeze punk!' 'Walk away now and I'll forget this ever happened!' and 'Ten four. On my way now!' to make security think you're a REAL law man. If they think you're a genuine grown-up with the power of arrest they will leave you alone. If they think you are a child in disguise, however, they will find out by sitting on a Whoopee Cushion. Laugh and you are lost. Lose and nobody will ever find you again.

If you are approached by a wind up toy do not believe a word it says. It will be a wind up.

NEVER play cards with a ventriloquist's dummy in case you are forced to say: 'Show me your hand!' Children have been fed to the crows for less. Ventriloquists' dummies are notoriously touchy about being reminded that someone else has got a hand in their existence

Never smile at a crocodile. (Now you've got me doing it!)

Alternatively, fill in this crossword, pop it into a bottle, drop it in a lava stream and hope that somebody finds it before the glass melts.

ACROSS
1. Nightmare without end has quiet scream (4)
2. Back of foot missing middle is short of money for aid (4)
DOWN
1. Greeting without lo adds small sounding vegetable for assistance (4)
2. Man followed by record shouts this (4)

WELCOME TO
THE HOTHELL DARKNESS
BREAKFAST 7.30AM - 9.30AM.

AT HOME, ANY TEDDY BEARS CAUGHT HIDING IN A PILLOWCASE WILL BE TAKEN AWAY AND HUNG, DRAWN AND QUARTERED BEFORE BEING RETURNED IN A PLASTIC BAG. ANY GUEST CAUGHT WITH A PILLOWCASE, OR FOR THAT MATTER A PILLOW, WILL BE FLOGGED SIX TIMES AFTER THE EARLY MORNING PSYCHIC HEALING SESSION IN THE NO-LEIKI ALTERNATIVE THERAPY CENTRE, WHERE ALTERNATIVE THERAPIES SUCH AS HEDGEHOG SKIN SCRUBS, HOT STONE HEAD MASSAGES AND ACUTELYPAINFULPUNCTURE ARE AVAILABLE 24/7. THESE ARE THE ODDS OF YOU GETTING OUT ALIVE.

The Night-night Porter

Well, look who it isn't! You keep getting away from me, you little devil, but not this time. This time I've made everything just the way you like it so you won't want to go.

You've got a choice of rooms: **The Gingerbread Suite** in which every item in the room is edible (including YOU, which gives the cockroaches something to get excited about) or **The Ghost Guest Room** in which I have stored some of the finest examples of ghosts known to grave-robbers: **Hairy Harry** who uses your hair to wipe his bottom; **Pukin' Petronella** who swallowed rat poison and can't keep her last supper down (a rather putrid Fricassee of Rat); and **Fletch the Finger-counter** who sits on the end of the bed counting his fingers. Sadly for you he thinks he should have eleven, so each time he discovers there's one missing he takes one from the person nearest to him. Oh, and **Eyeball Annie**. Whatever she sees she wants and whatever she wants she has. So never look her in the eye, especially when she's prodding around with her FONDUE FORK!

Before you can stay for ever I need to establish that you're as BAD as you look. Last thing I want is you coming back to me later complaining that you don't deserve the inhospitality of the Hothell Darkness!

ANSWER TRUTHFULLY

1. Your granny gives you a present for Christmas, but there is a notice on the box stating BATTERIES NOT INCLUDED and she has

forgotten to buy you any. Do you steal the batteries from her pacemaker?

2. Have you ever snapped a book's spine? Did it make you feel sinisterly powerful and send you scurrying out to look for other vulnerable titles?

3. Have you ever wished upon a star then ducked under the police cordon and shot him with your peashooter?

4. Could you fill a hamster with concrete and bury it under the patio? (If the answer is yes, see me afterwards)

5. If you were playing a War Game with tin soldiers would you use a blow torch to nuke your opponents?

You've answered **YES** to all of these questions, haven't you? **CONGRATULATIONS!** You will be staying in the Hothell Darkness for ever. In case you're worried that staying in this five-star pit is going to be a bit like hanging around the house getting bored on a wet Sunday, you'd be wrong. It doesn't rain down here.

Besides, there's plenty to do while you're slowly rotting in this hothell. You could always join our **DEADLY TOY-MAKERS' CLUB** which does such a useful job clearing the Earth of bad children. It meets every day in the sweatshop between the hours of 5.00 am – 11.00 pm. Help manufacture cute but deadly toys such as the racing-car game **SCALECTRIFY!** With just a couple of crossed-wires in the handset, it's perfect for electrocuting little boys!

Help build our special edition Cluedo with real murder weapons.

and our rocking horse called Icarus that unscrews its hooves from its rockers. grows wings and flies straight into the sun with screaming children stuck to its Velcro saddle. Or chop-along-a-CHOPERATION: where we cleverly substitute plastic surgical instruments for real ones thus ensuring that kids save me the time and bother by chopping each other up on the kitchen table!

So do something useful with your afterlife. And why not bring some hot tea and a packet of Rich Tea biscuits and relax with a copy of our visitor's book (or as I prefer to call it The Book of Grizzly Tales) in which you can read all about the naughty antics of our other guests.

I nearly forgot; if you're bringing stuff with you. pop in some strawberry flavoured throat sweets for the roaring sore throat you'll get from all the screaming you'll be doing!

Aaaaaaaaaaaaaaaaargh!

The naughty children in these tales all live in the Doll's House. It's a tiny extension out the back of the Hothell Darkness what I reserve for guests who think that toys are there to be abused. If they haven't stolen toys or broken them. these horrible brats have beaten them up.

Hello, I'm your friend!

Not a sausage!

tap tap tap tap tap tap tap tap tap tap tap tap

Why do boys have sticky fingers?

I CAN NOW. I CAN!

Bzzzzzzzzzzzzzzzzzzzzzzzzzzzzzzzzzzzzzzzzzz!

Ooh, there they are now my little Dollies, as I like to call them. Once they get down here, I give them a taste of their own medicine by treating them no better than toys. When they break they stay broken, when I grow tired of their faces or my three-headed pet dog, Seborrhoea, shreds them with his teeth. I chuck them in the bin. Easy come, easy go! Who needs two legs or a head when one stump and a severed neck will do?

Now you're scared of reading further. Oh go on! What have you got to lose? Apart from your life, and the majority of your body parts. Exactly!

Jealousy is a terrible sickness for which there is no cure but self-control. Greed, on the other hand, or the acquisition of possessions that do not belong to you, can be cured in several ways. ASBOs are occasionally handy, prison sentences can sometimes work, and chain gangs are not without their merits, but there is one cure for greed that never fails. Intestines stuffed with blood and meat, or should I say . . . SAUSAGES!

This is a tale about a greedy little boy who wanted other peoples' toys so BADLY that he forgot the golden rule . . .

THE GOLDEN RULE

A THIEF SHOULD NEVER PLAY WITH TOYS
THAT STILL BELONG TO BUTCHER BOYS
FOR IN THOSE FINGERS BLOODY RED
NOW POKING THROUGH A PIGLET'S HEAD
THERE LIVES A TWITCH THAT MUST BE FED
TO FIND THE THIEF AND CUT HIM DEAD!

I LOVE it when children forget the rules!

The Night-flight Porter

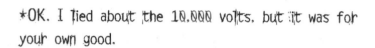

*OK. I lied about the 10.000 volts. but it was for your own good.

THE BUTCHER BOY

There was a windswept town on the Yorkshire Moors called Hockengristle: a slate-grey valley town; a dull, damp spot surrounded by sucking bogs and quicksand. For those poor souls born in Hockengristle there was no way out. Just the fog and the fear and for the lucky few, a poor quality satellite television service.

There was also a famous butcher's shop. It stood on the High Street amidst its dull counterparts; a shining, prosperous business with a striped red awning and, fresh every morning in the window, trays of white bones and puddling red meat. Any butcher will tell you that the fresher the meat the better the business.

The business was run by three generations of the same family, the Knucklebones. There was grandfather Gideon, ninety years with blood on his hands; *his* son Chopper, fifty years with one eye and three fingers; and *his* son, Chuck, eleven years wise with a taste for liver and heart. The strange thing was, even though all three were still alive, they had *never* been seen together.

In the same town, but born of different stock, lived a boy called Gilbert Leek. He came from a family with money. His mother had inherited a sugar plantation when she was twenty-one and his father lived off the income. The first words that Gilbert ever spoke were not 'mummy', 'daddy' or 'doggy', but 'Give me a thousand pounds.' Luckily, his mother had the sense to say 'no'. Unlike Gilbert she had learned that money had to be respected first and spent second, not the other way round.

Hello, I'm your friend!

You're not popular. Emily

By the time he was three, Gilbert had still not received a penny and was fed up. In Gilbert's world the most popular child was the child who had all the newest toys that nobody else could afford. If he wanted to become top dog in his playgroup, therefore, he needed a big pot of cash to *buy* the newest toys. But he didn't get it. By the age of eight, after five years of wheedling, he finally convinced his parents to give him one pound a week pocket money, but it was still not enough. Come his eleventh birthday, he was so fed up with being poor that he devised a plan to make himself an overnight fortune. Ironically, the first thing he had to do was spend the £121.50 that he'd saved from his pocket money on a digital camera.

The following morning, he did not come down for breakfast. His mother was calling out his name in the hallway when a ransom note, written using letters cut from a newspaper, plopped through the letterbox.

GILBERT IS SAFE . . .
FOR THE TIME BEING!
PAY US £100,000 OR YOU WILL NEVER SEE YOUR SON ALIVE AGAIN. IF YOU DO NOT BELIEVE WE ARE SERIOUS, TAKE A LOOK AT THIS PHOTOGRAPH OF GILBERT WHICH WE HAVE TAKEN THIS MORNING IN HIS PRISON CELL WHERE WE ARE HOLDING HIM CAPTIVE. NOW, PAY UP, YOU MEANIES!

There was a photograph of Gilbert standing forlornly against a wall holding that morning's newspaper. In a flash, Gilbert's parents rushed upstairs to Gilbert's bedroom where, to their horror, they found an open window and evidence of a fierce struggle.

'He really has been kidnapped!' gasped his mother, clutching her heart and swooning into Gilbert's father's arms. Unfortunately he was looking at the photograph at the time and she fell on the floor.

'Look at that!' he cried, pointing at the wallpaper in Gilbert's bedroom. 'The room he's being held in has exactly the same wallpaper as *this* room.'

'Isn't life strange?' said his mother, rubbing the bump on her head. And they hurried off to the bank to withdraw the money to have their son released.

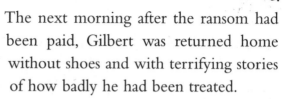

* * *

The next morning after the ransom had been paid, Gilbert was returned home without shoes and with terrifying stories of how badly he had been treated.

'They stole my trainers,' he cried, 'forced me to eat tinned fruit and wouldn't let me watch the telly!' His parents were shocked and made a fuss of their precious son, unaware that nestling in the waistband of his underpants, next to the £121.50 digital camera (with built-in timer for perfect self-portraits), was a large wad of cash that would change Gilbert's life forever!

Suddenly, the world was Gilbert's oyster. He had everything he wanted; more money than he could ever dream of, money with which he could buy all the latest toys to become the envy of his school friends.

'The more you flash your cash around, the more people like you,' he told his teddy bear the next morning. 'It's a jealousy thing.' He was living proof that money can buy you anything – skateboards, trainers, mobile phones, even friends! What no one tells you, however, is that money can also buy you a one way ticket to a poor man's picnic with the worms!

Is that clear enough for you? If not, try this: The reckless purchasing of toys as status symbols can sometimes lead to an early grave.

* * *

Now that Gilbert was the richest boy in the school he wanted everyone to *know* it.

When Michael Turner brought his new chess set in to Show and Tell, Gilbert asked to be excused, and seconds later, after speeding to the shops, returned with a new *automatic* chess set, complete with self-moving pieces and a hologrammatic Grand Master to teach him how to win. Needless to say, everyone wanted to play with Gilbert's set and poor Michael Turner was left to lug his ordinary board home on his own. When Phoebe Clawhammer brought a kite into the playground, Gilbert rushed out and bought a hang glider, which he landed right on top of Phoebe's kite thereby breaking its back. When Terence Filch bought an MP3 player, Gilbert bought his own indie band, which he drove around town on a flat-bed trailer so that his music could follow him wherever he went. When Chloe Swinton Berry trotted in to school on her new pony, Gilbert bought a jet-black stallion called Granite and frightened her pony away. And when Peaches Mulhoon and Ahmed Iqbal bought a beautiful wooden yacht with their joint pocket money, Gilbert bought a remote controlled, steel-hulled US warship, complete with launch pad for gung-ho presidential visits, which he carved through the middle of their yacht, sinking it without trace.

The truth was Gilbert could not bear anyone else to be the centre of attention and used his money to run them and their toys out of town. Then, one day, just after Christmas, Chuck, the butcher boy, brought his new bicycle into school. The Knucklebones had just sold three thousand turkeys and were rolling in festive fivers, so it was the newest bike on the market with all the extras; including friction-free paint (as used on the space shuttle), automatic gearing, on-board games console, and a uniquely-moulded gel saddle to banish bum blisters.

Gilbert took one green-eyed look at this magnificent machine and, more importantly, at the admiring looks that its owner was receiving, and dashed into town to buy himself something better. But, even though he rushed into fifty different shops Gilbert could not buy a better bike anywhere. For the first time since the hostage scam, Gilbert's money could *not* buy him the toy that he wanted.

* * *

By the time Gilbert got back to school he was cross. When he saw that Chuck and his bike were still the centre of attention it loosened most of the screws in his brain! Gilbert did not like being second best. It steamed him up and warped his thoughts until they were as twisted as Elastoman's leotard. If Gilbert couldn't *buy* a better bike, he'd *steal* the best and claim it as his own.

This is a common ailment known as Going-Toy-Tonto (or Insanitoy) when the longing for a toy overtakes a child's NEED for it. I've got a three-year old girl in the Dolls' House called Louisa — at least she *was* three when she entered The Darkness. Silly girl stole a doll from a birthday party. because she couldn't bear to leave it behind. She's been wishing she *had* ever since . . . It was her forty-third birthday last week. her joints are rusting and strands of her long nylon hair have just started falling out of the holes in her head!

He waited until the bell had sounded for the end of lunch, registered his name with his form teacher, then slipped out of a window at the back of the classroom, legged it into town and bought a pair of bolt croppers from the locksmiths. Half an hour, later he shinned over the railings and ducked down behind the bike shed. He had five minutes until school finished for the day. All it took was one snip through the steel padlock and Chuck's super-bike changed owners. One sinful snip before Gilbert rode it home and hid it in his bedroom.

There was an almighty fuss at the end of school when Chuck came out to find that his pride and joy had gone. He rushed home in tears and told his father, Chopper, who went back to school on his own to look for clues. He couldn't find any, returned home empty-handed and reported the theft to *his* father, Gideon. The oldest Knucklebone returned to the scene of the crime without his son or grandson. He didn't say a word. He sniffed the ground where the bike had stood and ran his tongue along the metal stand where its front wheel had been parked. Then he stood up with a no-good twinkle in his eye.

'Well?' said the local policeman, who had opened a half-hearted investigation that was rapidly going nowhere. 'What have you found?'

'Sausages,' said the old butcher. 'I taste sausages.'

That night, as an old-fashioned fog swirled down the street where Gilbert lived and an old-fashioned hound howled at the fuzzy moon, an old-fashioned bicycle bell jerked Gilbert from his sleep. It rang outside to a regular beat. *Ding ding! Ding ding!* It sounded just like the bell of a corpse cart during the time of the Black Death.

When he peered out of his window Gilbert could see very little. Along the pavement, the street lamps lit up the curtain of fog every thirty yards. In and out of these columns of light rode a boy in tweed jacket and cap sitting astride an old-fashioned butcher's bicycle. The street, the fog, the bike, the boy – it was like a scene from a Victorian picture postcard. When the bicycle pulled up outside Gilbert's house, he saw the boy's face for the first time.

It was Chuck. He looked up at Gilbert's bedroom window, causing Gilbert to duck behind his curtain hoping that he hadn't been seen. He waited long enough for Chuck to have moved on before daring to look out again. But the bicycle was still there, and Chuck had pulled out a metal object from the basket on the handlebars. It glinted in the streetlight as he drew back his arm and hurled the silver missile at the window. Gilbert threw himself across the floor as a butcher's cleaver smashed through the glass and embedded itself in the wall over his bed. There was a note pinned to the wall by the point of the cleaver. **WHERE IS MY BIKE?** it said, in ink the colour of ruby-red blood.

Peculiarly, Gilbert was not scared. Chuck was down there in the street, the stolen bike was up in the bedroom with Gilbert. Unless Chuck could jump twenty feet in the air, hover like a hummingbird and see the evidence through the bedroom window, how could he prove that Gilbert was in possession of his bike? It was impossible. Emboldened by this thought, Gilbert leaned out through the hole in the window and shouted, 'What bike?' But the stupid boy was shouting to himself, because the butcher boy and the butcher's bike had disappeared.

* * *

Gilbert checked over his shoulder, then behind the door and underneath his wardrobe before returning to bed. There was nobody there, so why was he suddenly feeling nervous? A faint, two-wheeled shadow rippled across the wall as he pulled back the bedclothes and prepared to jump in. But somebody was already in there; a boy in tweed jacket and cap.

'Chuck!' shrieked Gilbert. 'What do *you* want?'

'I've come for my son's bike,' said the red-cheeked boy, swinging his legs over the side of the mattress and standing up.

'Your *son's* bike!' exclaimed Gilbert. 'You haven't got a son.'

The boy laughed: a slow, mechanical laugh that drove shivers down Gilbert's spine. 'Who are you?' he trembled as Chuck wiped his bloody butcher's hands on Gilbert's duvet. '*What* are you?'

Chuck stretched his hand across his face and took hold of his own ear. Then, with a sharp tug, he tore off his face. There was no blood, just the nauseating sound of ripping flesh.

'I'm my own daddy,' he said, revealing Chopper's fifty-year-old face underneath. '*And* my own son.' Like a layered Russian doll, Chopper then tore off *his* face to expose the yellow skin and wrinkled features of Grandpa Gideon beneath.

Gilbert thought his heart had stopped. 'This isn't possible,' he whimpered. 'I don't understand.'

'We're a very close family,' said Gideon. 'We can trace our line right back to the Victorians and everyone knows how strict the Victorians were. "Children should be seen and not heard" is what they always used to say, although I must admit to a slight personal difference on that one. Me, I prefer, *not* seen and not heard, except when they're sizzling.' Gilbert made a dash for the door but the old man leapt nimbly in front of him. 'We've been butchering in Hockengristle for three generations. Looking after the neighbourhood, you might say. Clearing it of undesirables. If it's meat you want disposing of come to Knucklebones!'

'What does that mean?' whispered Gilbert, fearing the reply.

'It means you shouldn't have stolen my grandson's bike.'

'It's over there . . .' squeaked the boy. 'Take it.'

But Chuck's grandfather wasn't interested in the bike. 'Bikes are ten a penny,' he said. 'Good fresh meat,

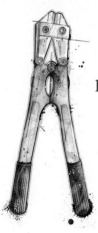

on the other hand, is priceless!'

'I'll pay you!' cried Gilbert. 'I've got loads of money. Have it all.'

'Don't want money.' The butcher smiled.

'I only wanted the bike so people would like me best at school,' wailed Gilbert. 'Take it and I'll give you whatever you want to go away.' But there are some things even money can't buy, as Gilbert was just about to find out.

'What I really want—' Gideon Knucklebone smiled again, pulling out the cleaver from the wall '—is *you!*' Which was pretty much everything that Gilbert didn't want to hear.

If you know of a toy that has created this much terror I'd LOVE to hear all the gory details. Send picture and postcard to:

Terror-Time Toys
The Hothell Darkness
On the Far Side of Fear
But Coming Soon To Somewhere Very Near You!

The next morning, Chuck rode his new bike into school, and distributed Gilbert's expensive toys to all of the children whom Gilbert had humiliated and upset. Michael was given the automatic chess set, Phoebe the hang-glider, Terence his own band, Chloe the stallion, and Peaches and Ahmed a US warship.

Meanwhile, in the High Street, a butcher's shop was opening for business. There was a new sign in the window:

MEAT TO DIE FOR

'Morning Mr Knucklebone,' said Gilbert's mother.

'Morning, Mrs Leek,' said Grandfather Gideon. 'Have they found young Gilbert yet?'

'Still looking, Mr Knucklebone. He'll be out meeting someone and forgot to tell us.'

'Or being meated,' chuckled the butcher.

'Quite,' smiled Gilbert's mother, not fully understanding what the old man meant. 'Can you recommend anything today?'

'I've got some freshly made sausages, if you're interested.'

'Ooh, sausages! It would be a sin to refuse them,' she smiled. 'You do make the best sausages in the world, Mr Knucklebone!' Gideon plunged his fingers into the meat on the tray and held up a handful.

'We aim to please,' said the butcher boy, 'we *always* aim to please.'

What I want to know is, if Gideon, Chopper and Chuck believe that meat is murder, why aren't they vegetarian? It's not as if they couldn't still have sausages, because they could have *vegetarian* sausages – one part vegetable, one part cereal, one part vegetarian. Best use of vegetarians, in my opinion.

I CAN NOW! I CAN NOW

You won't be able to for much longer if you don't put a sock in it, Calloway!

Now, I know I'm stating the obvious, but children love toys. It's the same with sweets. So if you want to get close to children without them knowing they're in danger toysRbest! When I creep around the world on my Press Ganging trips to fill any empty rooms I might have, I always use toys to trap my victims. The trick is getting the toy CLOSE to your target before springing your surprise! Surprises like the elasticated intestines that burst out the belly of a cuddly clown and lasso the bawling brat round its neck; or the poisoned pancakes in Little Miss Perfect's 'Play Kitchen', or the fish hooks which crawl out the telescope and bury themselves in the cocky astrologer's eyeballs! Boiled sweets are easy to spike too. You just crack them open, stick a dead Malaria Fly in the middle and superglue the two halves back together again.

Of course, the toy that children love most is the teddy bear. Who can blame them? Teddies are soft and cuddly, their lips are always ready for a kiss and they're the best listeners in the world, apart from sharks of course. Sharks are GREAT listeners, cruising the bottom of the ocean listening for swimmers! One splash and WOOOOOMPH! All teeth and tearing. Imagine bedtime if a teddy bear did that. You'd never get any sleep at all, would you? Because you'd NEVER know . . .

'Night-night, sleep tight, hope your teddy doesn't bite!'

Why do boys have sticky fingers?

Not a sausage!

I CAN NOW. I CAN!

Hello, I'm your friend!

Bzzzzzzzzzzzzzzzzzzzzzzzzzzzzzzzzzzzzzzzzzzzzzz!

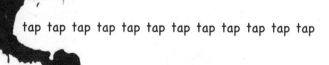

tap tap tap tap tap tap tap tap tap tap tap tap

THE
BUGABOO
BEAR

Emily Stiff was a pink little girl with her hair in
bunches and everything ever so dainty. She walked
on her tippy-toes wherever she went, which made
her legs ache like billio, but it was
worth every cramp and seizure, because
passers-by thought she was a ballerina.
When she danced down the pavement,
drivers would stop their cars in the
middle of the road to applaud her
twinkling feet, and the traffic
wardens, who had stopped to give
tickets to the stationary cars, would shout 'Bravo!'
and throw her flowers!

Emily Stiff liked being a girl. She liked looking
pretty and playing with dolls and cooking
shortbread with her granny. She liked smelling soft
towels and cuddling her duvet and picking dainty

flowers. She liked chocolate and cherries and ice cream sorbets, but she *loved* her teddy. She had bought it because it had the cutest smile in the toy shop, and when she got it home she called it Cutie.

Cutie had a mop of spiky hair on the top of his head, a floppy fringe, gentle green eyes and a voice inside his chest that said over and over again, 'Hello, I'm your friend.'

'And I'm yours too,' cried Emily Stiff, hugging her bear like a hot-water bottle and whispering in its ear, 'I love you, Cutie. Now, you promise you won't tell, will you? It's our little secret. Just you and me. Together.'

For all her pink prettiness Emily Stiff was hiding a dark secret.

Well, everyone does, don't they? Don't they? I certainly do. I . . . actually, if I was to tell you my secret I'd have to show you a certain part of my anatomy, and then I'd have to kill you . . . slowly.

Emily's secret was locked away in her toy cupboard, behind a 'N⊕ Entry' sign and a skull-and crossbones sticker that promised INSTANT DEATH to anyone who trespassed. Emily's parents used to think they were going mad when they heard voices coming from that cupboard — faint little voices, scared little voices, sad little voices that whispered and wailed, 'Help! Let us out!'

tap tap tap tap tap tap tap tap tap tap

No. They DIDN"T type their words. Eric.

They tried to open the cupboard to see what was crying inside, but Emily had the key hidden in her sock. Only Cutie knew what horrors lay behind that cupboard door, because Emily had told him. She thought that Cutie was a toy and didn't have the words to tell. What Emily didn't know was that Cutie was a Bugaboo Bear.

A Bugaboo Bear is like a samurai warrior. It's an ordinary bear that becomes *extra*ordinary when it trains to uphold the honour of Bugaboo through the art of fear and retribution. The word Bugaboo comes from **'bug'**, as in *something scary that you hope you'll never meet* and **'boo!'** as in *Aaaaagh! I've just met something scary!* After training, a Bugaboo Bear can think for itself. Its glassy eyes can see and observe its owner's behaviour. Its sleeping brain can switch itself on when direct action is required. Not for them worn elbows and feet, ripped ears or torn limbs; Bugaboo Bears are trained to outlast their owners, which is bad news for bad children like Emily Stiff!

* * *

When Cutie first came to live with Emily Stiff, it was a marriage made in heaven. Emily treated Cutie like a baby. They cuddled up in bed together, read books together, watched television together. They were inseparable. But one day, in something of a sulky strop, because she couldn't do her homework, Emily sat Cutie on her desk and asked him a question.

'I hate maths,' she said, sucking the rubber on the end of her pencil. 'It's stupid adding and stuff, and I'm never going to use it when I grow up.' Cutie smiled just like he always did. 'What's seven times nine, Cutie?'

'Hello, I'm your friend.' This was all Cutie ever said.

'No, seven times nine!' Emily needed the answer now. 'Say something else for a change!' she shouted, shaking the bear by its shoulders. 'What's seven times nine? COME ON! SEVEN TIMES NINE!'

'Hello, I'm your friend.'

Emily saw red, picked Cutie up by one leg and hurled him at the wall. That night, the Bugaboo Bear slept in a cold draught on the floor.

* * *

The next day, when Emily was given a detention for not completing her maths homework, she blamed the stupid bear. She cursed the picture of him that she kept in her pencil case, before tearing it into a hundred tiny pieces and throwing them out of the window.

Later that evening, as they usually did, Emily's parents laid an extra place at the supper table for Cutie. When Emily appeared, however, she had left her teddy bear upstairs.

'Is Cutie asleep?' fussed her mother. 'I've cooked a little extra for him.'

'Is something the matter with your brain?' sneered Emily. 'Since when did toy bears eat food? He doesn't have a stomach, you know.'

'But I thought he was your baby,' said a startled Mrs Stiff.

'Not any more,' came the ice-cold reply.

'Oh dear,' joked her father. 'Have you two had an argument?'

'Listen!' shouted Emily. 'If you love Cutie so much, *you* go and get him! But he won't eat anything, because he's stuffed with sawdust, his eyes are made out of glass, and that stupid voice of his is from a battery-operated box in his chest.'

Her parents were shocked. Not half as much as Cutie, who didn't know what he'd done to offend Emily. He only wanted to please her.

'Hello, I'm your friend,' he said later that night when Emily climbed into bed.

'Oh not again!' she groaned. 'If you don't shut up, I'll lock you up in the toy cupboard.' Then she tossed him out of bed and left him to sleep upside down on his head.

Why do boys have sticky fingers?

Because I put glue in your pockets, you numpty!

Now that Emily Stiff had decided that her teddy bear was not a baby she grew bored with it. She could have put it away in a box and stored in on a top shelf until she had children of her own to play with it, but Emily was not like that. She turned nasty. She stopped being Cutie's friend and became his torturer instead.

She tied him to a chair and cut his hair with kitchen scissors. She gave him pigtails and pony tails and a green Mohican with a bottle of food dye.

She opened her bedroom window and tested him to see if he could fly. She hurled Cutie into the rain and watched him nosedive into a puddle of mud.

'Hello, I'm your friend.' coughed Cutie's automated voice.

'Why would I want a friend who can't fly?' Emily shouted out of her window. 'You're useless!'

Then she ran a bath for Cutie. Instead of washing off the mud, however, she gave the bear lessons in underwater swimming, pinning him down on the bottom of the bath by lying a brick across his chest.

'Hello, I'm your friend,' bubbled the teddy bear's cry for help.

'You wish!' hissed Emily Stiff. Then she rushed the bear down to the kitchen and dried him out in the oven.

* * *

That night, a slightly crisp and gently smoking teddy bear sat slumped in a chair on a pile of little girl's clothes. It was watching Emily Stiff when its sleeping brain switched itself on. As midnight chimed, its glassy eyes rolled in their sockets and glowed bright red as the Bugaboo Bear put its training into action and planned its revenge!

THINGS YOU CAN DO TO MAKE TOYS MORE DEADLY

**Another good idea from
The Deadly Toy-makers' Club
Number 423**

Fill a football with high explosives

The next day Emily Stiff decided to punish the bear for being her friend. Teddy bears hated the cold so she took him on a trip to the North Pole.

'You're going to like it in here,' she said as she opened the freezer door and sat Cutie down on a block of ice. 'You can learn how to ice skate.'

'Hello, I'm your friend.'

'Just shut up about that, all right? Do you know how to ice skate? Of course you don't, because you don't have a brain. You're just a big bag of sawdust, aren't you? Watch.' And she showed the bear how to do it. 'This is skating. Like this.' She slid around the kitchen floor in her socks, but Cutie stared straight ahead and ignored her. 'Oi, cloth-ears!' she yelled. 'Are you listening to a word I'm saying?' She twisted the teddy's ear as hard as she could. 'Have you got it?'

'Hello, I'm your friend.' Emily Stiff exploded.

'No you're not! Not anymore! Now stay in there and do something interesting for once!' In a peak of temper she pushed the bear to the back of the freezer, slammed the door and stomped away to read a book.

When she returned, ten minutes later, the North Pole was a noise-free zone.

'What's going on in there?' she said, with her ear pressed up against the door. 'How's the ice skating coming on?'

'Hello,' whispered a frozen voice. 'I'm your friend.' She tugged open the door to find Cutie sitting in exactly the same position as she'd left him.

Apart from his lips turning blue nothing had changed. This was the final straw! Her disobedient teddy bear had openly defied her orders!

'Look at you!' she screamed. 'You're so naughty! You've just been sitting there, when you should have been doing what I told you to do. What's wrong with you?'

'I'm cold,' said Cutie, stopping Emily Stiff dead in her tracks. The hairs on the back of her neck stood to attention as if a ghost had walked right through her.

'What did you say?'

'I'm cold.'

When the Bugaboo Bear spoke for the first time, Emily Stiff caught her breath. When it spoke for the second time she thought her heart had stopped beating. But it hadn't, or she wouldn't have been able to do what she did next.

* * *

She became a doctor, a surgeon to be precise. Dr Stiff could not have her teddy bear talking back, so she prepared her bed for an emergency operation. She covered her duvet in a green towel and moved her desktop lamp onto the bedside table to illuminate the patient's chest. Then she laid Cutie down on the towel and picked up a pair of scissors.

'I haven't given you an anaesthetic,' she sneered gleefully, 'because I want you to *feel* everything I'm doing. The next time you decide to question my orders maybe you'll think twice!' Showing no fear, the Bugaboo Bear stared at the ceiling through glassy eyes while Emily plunged the scissors into its chest and made a long incision from neck to bellybutton. She peeled back the bear's fur and pulled out its stuffing. Underneath, wired up like a small metal heart, she found a tiny tape recorder which kicked off as she touched it.

'Hello, I'm your friend.'

She tore it out through the slit in the bear's chest, hurled it onto the floor and crushed it with the heel of her shoe.

'Ow!' cried the Bugaboo Bear, as she stamped on its voice box. 'That hurts!'

'Good!' shrieked Emily Stiff. 'I don't ever want to hear you again!'

Suddenly, in response to Cutie's distress calls, the wailing voices inside Emily's toy cupboard made themselves heard.

'This is how the monster treats us,' they cried. 'Fight back for all! Fight back and win the day!' Emily laughed and kicked the cupboard door.

'Fight back!' she mocked. 'This old rag!' Without his stuffing, Cutie was as floppy as a pyjama case. 'I'd like to see him try!' Then to make sure he wasn't going anywhere, she shoved her dead Ted in her sock drawer, slammed it shut and jumped into bed.

* * *

Later that night, while Emily slept deeply, the drawer creaked open. Two brown leather paws appeared over the top, then a shock of green hair. The Bugaboo Bear flopped out onto the floor and dragged itself across the carpet to the wastepaper bin where its stuffing had been discarded. Then it pushed the stuffing back inside its belly, stitched itself up and went to work with a fleck of cold steel in its eye and a wicked smile upon its face.

Using its mouthful of razor-sharp teeth, the

Bugaboo Bear chewed up all the wooden furniture in the bedroom and spat out the sawdust into a large pile on the rug in the middle of the floor. Then it dragged the rug to Emily Stiff's bedside, and while she snored, it poured the sawdust into her mouth until she was quite full up and *her* eyes were glassy. Then it stitched her mouth closed and dragged her downstairs like a sack. Bump! Bump! Bump! Bump! Her listless head banged on each step like a solitary drum beating a path to the gallows.

Outside it was a cold, starless night. The Bugaboo Bear struggled up the empty street with its heavy load, hugging the shadows so as not to be seen. A passing car's headlamps swung across its path, but did not stop. When it reached the doorway of The Charity Shop, the bear let go of Emily's feet and walked away, whispering under its breath, 'Goodbye, Emily Stiff, and good riddance.'

That's my kind of bear!

BZZZZZZZZZZZZZZZZZZZZZZZZZZZZZZZZZZZZZZZZZZZZZZZZZZZ

* * *

In the morning, when the two volunteers arrived to open up the shop, they found a life-sized doll blocking the door.

'Och, Elsie,' said the elder of the two Scottish sisters. 'Isn't that a big dolly?'

'Biggest I've ever seen,' said Elsie. 'Should fetch at least five pounds.' Then they dragged the doll indoors and sat it in the window with a sign around its neck:

FOR SALE:

WOULD SUIT LITTLE GIRL LOOKING FOR A FRIEND

'Oh, Daddy, please! I want it! I really, really do!'

Two hours later a little girl was tugging at her father's hand, trying to drag him off the pavement into the shop.

'All right, I'm coming,' he said. He bought her the big doll on the understanding that she would look after it.

'Of course I will,' she said. 'I always treat my toys well.'

More than could be said for *some* little girls!

44

So Emily Stiff became the little girl's best friend. At first it was a marriage made in heaven. The little girl treated Emily like a baby. They cuddled up in bed together, read books together, and watched television together. They were inseparable. Emily Stiff even helped the little girl with her homework.

Then one day, the little girl looked cross. There was no reason, she just didn't like her big doll anymore. She tied it to a chair and cut its hair with the kitchen scissors. That was the day, the day that history started to repeat itself, when Emily Stiff suddenly wished she'd treated her Bugaboo Bear better. But of course, she hadn't.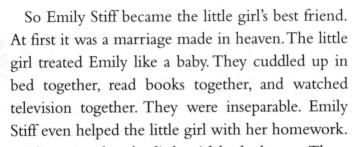

'Hello,' said Emily Stiff, hoping to stop the little girl from doing her harm. 'I'm your friend.'

'No, you're NOT!' growled the little girl. 'Let's play doctors and patients!'

In the meantime, while Emily Stiff had the stuffing knocked out of her, a teddy bear climbed into her bedroom through an open window. It ran across the carpet to the toy cupboard and unlocked the doors. The shelves were lined with every broken toy that Emily Stiff had ever abused.

'OK, toys!' said the Bugaboo Bear. 'You're free to go!'

<u>Beware of The Bear!</u>
If you've just been given a teddy bear,
Don't freeze its butt or cut its hair
Lest you shuld seal your mortal fate
And find out it's a Bugaboo too late!

Because the little girl turned Emily Stiff into Emily
Flop-All-Over-The-Place. I use her as a tea pot cover
in the Hothell kitchen. And after work I chuck her in
the toy cupboard in the doll's house. Every night
before I go to bed I check on her just to make sure
that the other toys are giving her a right good going-
over! In many ways I'm the Bugaboo Bear of the Hothell
Darkness. Show me a child who is naughty and rude and
I'll show them the terror!

Not a sausage!

Not a sausage, no — The Terror

Sometimes, bad children don't even have to be down
here to get the treatment. I shouldn't be telling you
this, because the thought that I might be creeping up
behind you at any time of night or day might TERRIFY
you, but many's the time I've sneaked up to your world
to have a bit of a laugh at your expense. Remember

that girl who kissed the animals in the zoo when the sign said **DON'T** and ended up with a tarantula stuck to the front of her face? That was me.

And it was me who did for that boy who was camping — the one who refused to even TASTE the food that his scout leader had spent hours cooking on the camp fire. It was me who I told the boy to slip the chow into his sock to make it LOOK like he'd eaten it when he hadn't. I forgot to mention was that it was Grizzly country and later that night two hungry bears ate his feet. Funny or what!!!

And it was also me who did for that cocky kid who went out stealing and thought the police could never catch him. It was ME who stitched him up like a kipper.

You must remember the story? The boy's name was Billy. The one with all those boys' toys, which is what made him think his crimes were undetectable.

WHAT ARE BOYS' TOYS?
EDUCATIONAL BIT

The expression Boys' Toys first appeared in a mediaeval poem called 'The Burglar of Bath' by full-time pig-squeezer and part-time playwright, Geoffrey Chancer.

'Boyes' toyes givve constabule no joyes!'

. . . which basically translates as: *Boys' toys prevent policemen from catching burglars.*

Boys' Toys aren't some sort of invisible pills that make a burglar vanish. Boys' Toys are toys owned by boys and can be ANYTHING ON THE PLANET, because boys can make toys out of bits of string, rubber bands, dead hedgehogs, and congealed balls of snot. They don't need dolls and fairy wings; give a boy a stick and he's happy — a bit like a dog. In fact, EXACTLY like a dog. A dog can make friends with a stick for life and a boy plays golf. I rest my case.

ANOTHER EDUCATIONAL BIT
Ever wondered what ASBO stands for?
Adrian Smith has BO, so stay away from him.

By the way, a leaflet to accompany this story, containing free advice for boys on how to make a proper career in burglary WITHOUT relying on Boys' Toys is available now from;

www.ivebeenknockingoffsweetshopssinceiwasanipperandimproudofit.com

priced extortionately to rip you off.

WHY BOYS MAKE BETTER BURGLARS

When Mr and Mrs Burglar were expecting their first child, Mrs Burglar turned to her husband, who had just climbed in through the bedroom window after a long night's burglarisation and said, 'Ronnie, I don't care if it's a boy or a girl. I just want it to be healthy.'

'Don't be daft!' said Mr Burglar, pulling off his stripy jumper and mask. 'It's gotta be a boy.'

'Why?'

'Crikey O'Riley, don't you know nuffink, you silly old teabag?' Moths flew up from his socks as he unlaced his boots. ''Cause boys make better burglars!'

Mrs Burglar couldn't see why this should be at all. Girls were just as good as boys. In most areas of life they were better, but she didn't like to talk about such things with Mr Burglar in case he broke the wedding china.

But for once, Mr Burglar knew his onions.

When the baby was born it was a boy, and they called him Billy. On the day that Billy Burglar left hospital, however, Mr Burglar was sentenced to do big bird for a botched-up bakery blag in Billericay. The policeman who caught him found him hiding in a bag of white flour.

'Ronnie Burglar!' he shouted. 'Consider yourself caught bread-handed!'

Mr Burglar tried to get away by waving his arms and pretending he was a ghost, but policemen are trained to have nerves of steel and the officer took no notice.

* * *

Mr Burglar didn't get out of prison until Billy was six months old, but on the day of his release, Mrs Burglar was banged up for swiping a swazzle from a

Punch and Judy entertainer. When questioned at the police station, she said, in strangely gruff voice that whizzed and wheezed exactly like the voice of Mr Punch, 'It wasn't me, Officer. I never done nothing!'

But she had, and Mrs Burglar didn't see Billy's sunny smile again until it was full of teeth.

Hello, I'm your friend!

Don't believe her. She only woke up because someone mentioned teeth!

In fact, the first time Billy saw his parents *together* was when he was three, at his little sister's first birthday party. Even then his father was only passing through. While Roxie Burglar was blowing out her candle, Billy's father was chased through the kitchen by eight policemen in size twelve boots.

'Take them off!' ordered Mrs Burglar when the policemen burst through the back door. 'I don't want your muddy footprints on my nice clean floor.' It was a good stalling tactic, but it didn't work. They caught Mr

Burglar and gave him 240 hours Community Service.

The point is that with parents like Mr and Mrs Burglar it was hardly surprising that Billy was a burglar too. The police knew he had *bad boy* in his blood from the moment he was born. That was why they kept a round-the-clock surveillance team on him from six hours old. And over the years they had a good deal of success, photographing each and every one of his misdemeanours.

When he was one, they snapped him nicking nappies from the hospital. When he was three, they caught him kidnapping ducks from the boating pond. When he was six they videotaped him pinching going-home presents from his best friend's party, and when he was nine they got him on camera half-hitching a Hammerstein out the window of his piano teacher's flat.

But they couldn't arrest him.

'Why?' asked Mrs Burglar holding the torch over the ground plans of the bank so that Mr Burglar could read them. 'Is it because he's a boy?'

'Nah, 'cause he's too young,' said Mr Burglar, picking up his pick-axe.

Mrs Burglar had never been very

good at understanding the law. 'So why do boys make better burglars?' she coughed, holding up the candle to the rock face so that Mr Burglar could see what he was hitting. He wiped the dust off his face and grinned.

'You'll see why,' he said, 'on the first day the coppers ask him to turn out his pockets.' Mrs Burglar, hated answers that didn't answer questions, but she knew when to hold her tongue and when to speak out; and underground, in the middle of tunnelling into a bank vault, was not the right time to press for an explanation.

Mrs Burglar did not have to wait long, however, before she understood what her husband meant.

* * *

It was Billy Burglar's tenth birthday. At six o'clock in the morning he ran into his parents' bedroom to receive his presents. His little sister Roxie had bought him a brick.

'It's smashing for smashing windows or standing on if you're keeping look out,' she said.

'It's brilliant,' said Billy. 'Thanks.' The parcel he got from his mum and dad was heavier. 'Is it an anchor?' he asked.

'It's not an anchor,' squealed his mum.

'Open it,' said Mr Burglar. So Billy did.

'Oh, it's beautiful!' he cried as he tore off the last strip of wrapping paper. 'It's just what I wanted. A grappling hook.'

'We thought you'd be pleased,' grinned Mrs Burglar, clutching her husband's hairy arm.

'Now, mind you get into trouble with that, Bill,' said Mr Burglar. 'I don't want you coming home with none of this *'I'm not strong enough to throw it up at a window, Dad!'*

'Yes.' Mrs Burglar winked. 'Go out there and make your mum and dad proud.'

'Now?' gasped Billy, his eyes wide with disbelief. 'You mean I can bunk off school?'

'Go on then!' smirked Mr Burglar, who rather liked playing the softie. 'After all, it *is* a special occasion.'

So while Billy Burglar should have been practising his ABC, he was sneaking through the undergrowth in the gardens of the nearby manor house, hurling his grappling hook onto a handy parapet and hauling himself in through a first-floor window.

This is where I came in. If Billy wasn't caught, because of his Boys' Toys, he wouldn't come down here into the Darkness and I'd be out of a job. So, while he was scaling the wall I sent my TWIN SHADOW into the Manor House AHEAD of him to empty some sweets into a bowl on a walnut bureau. Billy was so sure he COULDN'T BE CAUGHT that trapping him was as easy as taking a mobile phone off a ten-year-old!

Billy found himself in a swanky drawing room full of red velvet swags and gold-leaf pictures. His mouth dropped open when he saw what riches there were to burglarise. While he was standing there contemplating what to take first he helped himself to a plum sour from a bowl on a walnut bureau. He was sucking it quietly when the door burst open and he was confronted by the owner of the manor house, the Duchess.

'Put that plum sour down, burglar!'

'How did you know my name?' said Billy, cunningly spitting the evidence out of his mouth and hiding the sticky plum sour in his pocket.

'Give it back,' hollered the grey-haired vigilante, 'or I'll call the police!'

Billy laughed. He knew something that the Duchess didn't. A bit of wisdom about Boys' Toys that he'd picked up from his dad – that from the moment the police asked Billy to turn out his pockets they'd be on a hiding to nothing and Billy would be set free. So Billy was brave. 'Do what you like, lady; I ain't scared,' he said, ''cause boys make better burglars.'

Unfortunately for Billy, Duchesses make better thief-catchers, because as Billy made a run for it, the Duchess locked the double doors by shoving her knobbly walking stick through the door handles. Then she bashed him on the head with her fox fur stole until he gave in. Billy was stitched up like a kipper and carted off to the police station on suspicion of pilfering a plum sour.

1–0 to ME! What Billy didn't know was that I had dipped each of those plum sours in extra strong INVISO–GLUE. which even though it's made from old fish bones is tasteless and invisible to the naked eye.

* * *

'At last,' said Sergeant Rough as he slammed shut the door to the interview room. He'd been after Billy for years and this time he was positive he could make the charges stick. All he needed was the evidence – in other words, the half-sucked plum sour. 'We got you bang to rights, Billy Burglar. Now, turn out your pockets.'

'OK,' said Billy, fearlessly (because of you-know-what). 'Ready?' Then he proceeded to empty the objects out of his pockets one by one; objects that only a boy would play with.

**A ball of string with a mouldy old
conker on the end.
A scrunched-up sweet paper with a
dried ladybird inside.
A magnetic robot.
A bent spoon.
A pair of yellow pants.
A paperclip.
Some chipped marbles.
A table tennis ball.
A broken shoe horn.
Several playing cards.
A mouse.
Some garden twine.**

Some headphones.
Two rusty penknives.
The dried skeleton of a frog.

'That's disgusting!' cried the Sergeant. 'How much more stuff have you got in those pockets of yours?'

'Plenty,' said Billy. 'You ain't seen nothing yet!' And he continued to empty the Boys' Toys out of his pockets onto the table.

A jar of live spiders.
A brown apple core wrapped in silver foil.
A cuddly toy.
A model Aston Martin with ejector seat.
An old bus ticket containing a design for
a Wasp Mangler ...

And so it went on.

An hour later, the table was piled high with Billy's stuff. The Sergeant had taken the weight off his feet and was sitting down, but Billy had only just started.

A catapault.
A Slinky.
A bundle of twigs held together with
a pipe cleaner.

Worms.
A box of bogeys.
A pot of enamel paint.
A magnifying glass.
A felt-tipped pen.
One dead stag beetle covered in Formula One
stickers.
A pair of knotted laces.
Eight World Cup trading cards.
An old sandwich filled with squashed flies.

'Shall I keep going?' asked Billy with a cheeky
smile. The sergeant, grimaced, took off his jacket
and nodded, so Billy carried on producing his toys.

Half a tennis ball.
A matchbox containing a leaf collection.
A piece of paper rolled into a funnel.
A bone from a mouse's leg.
Six keys on a Harry Snotter keyring.
A pair of miniature maracas filled with toenail
clippings.
A cereal bar with a flag on top.

'There's more in your pockets than I was
expecting,' sighed the Sergeant.

'It's only Boys' Toys,' said Billy smugly. 'All the essential stuff what every boy needs to enjoy himself!' And off he went again.

A plastic Ork.
Three battery powered calculators.
A pawn from a game of chess.
A bicycle pedal.
A tube of superglue with finger skin attached.
An electronic pet.
Mouldy cheese with the face of Elvis Presley on it.
A cowboy gun.
A snorkel and mask . . .

Three hours had passed. The table was groaning under the weight of Billy's toys, which had spilled over onto the floor and were touching the ceiling.

An inky-eyed joke telescope.
A whoopee cushion.
A pair of black leather golfing gloves.
A holey sock with moths living in it (like father like son).
Two tissues
And an iPod.

Suddenly the door burst open. Billy froze with his hand in his pocket. Standing in the doorway was the prim and proper Chief Inspector, a stickler for detail and a man of impeccable neatness.

'What is going on in here?' he yelled.

'Just checking this lad's pockets for a stolen Plum Sour, sir!' said the Sergeant, leaping to attention.

'Well, find it and charge him!' bellowed his superior. 'Just stop making such a mess of my police station!' So the search for the plum sour continued and Billy produced things from his pockets that he hadn't seen in years.

**A feeding bottle.
A musical mobile.
A rattle
And an old nappy.**

Two hours after that, with the police station bulging at the seams from the sheer quantity of boy junk, Billy Burglar produced the final object from the very bottom of his pocket. It was a Venus flytrap. The Chief Inspector had had enough.

'I hate boys and their bottomless pockets!' he screamed. 'Get him and his Boys' Toys out!'

'But we haven't found the Plum Sour yet, sir,'

protested the Sergeant.

'I don't care! I can't move in my own station. Out! Now!'

* * *

So you see, Billy's dad was right; boys *do* make better burglars. Thanks to his chock-a-block pockets Billy was free, because Sergeant Rough couldn't find the evidence he needed to charge him. Or rather Billy *would* have been free if he hadn't decided, rather stupidly, to blow a raspberry at the policemen to celebrate his victory. As he took his hand out of his pocket to place his thumb on his nose, the plum sour came with it stuck to the end of his index finger.

2–0! 3–0! 4–0! Whatever–0! Game, set and match to ME!

So glue's why boys have sticky fingers

Not much gets past you, does it, Mr Fishy-Fingers?

'Wait a minute!' said the Sergeant. 'What's that?'

Billy froze in disbelief as the Sergeant snatched the Plum Sour and licked it with the tip of his tongue.

'Is it sour?' asked the Chief Inspector, and with a look of joy Sergeant Rough replied, 'Well, it's not sweet.'

And that was how Billy Burglar got himself caught and sent to prison.

Or rather that's how *I* got Billy Burglar caught and sent to prison. Credit where credit's due!

One Sunday, when Mr Burglar turned up to visit his son in prison, he was full of remorse.

'It shouldn't have happened!' he said. 'They should *never* have found that plum sour. Not with a boy's pigsty pockets. Now if you'd been a girl like your sister, fair enough. She's got neat little girly pockets. There's no toys or bric-a-brac in them. If it had been *her* pockets, the police would have found the plum sour in no time at all!' He burst into tears and squeezed Billy's hand across the table. The prison guards watched closely in case he was slipping Billy a nail file. 'I'm sorry, son. I've let you down,' he sobbed. Billy didn't know what to say. He had never seen his father cry before. So his mum filled the silence with one of her sensible statements.

'Still,' she said. 'At least you've got your own room in here. That's nice.'

Then Mr and Mrs Burglar, and Billy's little sister Roxie, left Billy in prison to serve out the rest of his sentence, while they trotted outside into the sunshine with a whole new set of plans for making a dishonest living.

'Now then, Roxie,' said Mr Burglar, sitting the family down on a bench in a nearby park, 'did I ever tell you why girls make better shoplifters?'

The little girl shook her head.

'No? Right, your mum's got something for you.'

Mrs Burglar handed her daughter their present. 'It's a handbag, Roxie dear.'

'It's empty,' said Roxie.

'Yes,' said Mum.

'And it's *very* big!' said Roxie, which it was. It was huge.

'It is big, isn't it?' said Mr Burglar, smiling to himself. 'Now there's a very good reason for that, young lady . . .'

Do you know what that reason is? Because if you DO, *you* could be joining Billy and Roxie Burglar in The Darkness, ~~cell~~ room number 6785431. Oh yes, Billy's down here now. And Roxie was caught two weeks later nicking knickers from The Big Red Knicker Store, so she's down here with him. They're one big UNHAPPY family!

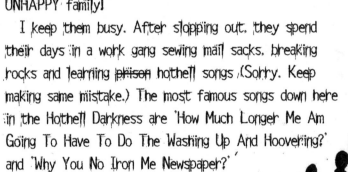

I keep them busy. After slopping out, they spend their days in a work gang sewing mail sacks, breaking rocks and learning ~~prison~~ hothell songs (Sorry. Keep making same mistake.) The most famous songs down here in the Hothell Darkness are 'How Much Longer Me Am Going To Have To Do The Washing Up And Hoovering?' and 'Why You No Iron Me Newspaper?'

THINGS YOU CAN DO TO MAKE TOYS MORE DEADLY

Another good idea from The Deadly Toy Makers Club

Number 68

Fit table tennis bats with teeth

> It takes a lot to scare me.

WHAT IT TAKES TO SCARE ME

1. Scissor pants
2. Aggressive spiders sleeping under cheese slices in the fridge
3. Fluegel Horns blown behind me without warning
4. This thought; If a glass of water turned into a glass of ClingFilm while I was drinking it I might be suffocated.
5. Forgetting to put my tights on during a bank robbery
6. Puppets that speak without a hand up their bottom
7. Angels with crossbows
8. Wearing contact lenses made out of tree bark
9. Magnetic ladybirds

Right now, however, I'm scared. If you read the next tale, you'll see why.

PUPPET ON A STRING

In a run-down town called Dollsville there is a theatre where no actors ever act. It stands amidst a swirl of rubbish on the corner of a deserted high street. It has a patched green copper dome and cracked concrete steps rising through Doric columns to a padlocked front of house. A faded poster, dominated by the silhouette of a wooden marionette, announces **'Coming Soon! Pinocchio!'** then slashed across the top in bright red paint, 'CANCELLED'.

After the accident two years ago the theatre was shut down. The lights were switched off, the make-up was thrown away, and the stage door was boarded up so that nobody could ever get inside again.

But it wasn't an accident. That's the whole point. They said that it *was* but it wasn't!

* * *

The boy was found hanging from the roof rafters. Not by the neck, for then he would have been dead, but by strings attached to his ankles, knees, elbows, hands, shoulders and head. He was a life-size string puppet, top-lit on the Toymaker's set, swaying gently like a parachutist caught in a tree. If you approached him, you could hear him whisper an endlessly repetitive mantra that sounded like a voodoo chant aimed at exorcising an evil spirit. All he could say was, 'I can now. I can. I can now. I can. I'll never say *can't* again.'

What a NICELY behaved boy. I hear you say. What lovely manners. So polite. But 'twas not always thus. Oh no! There was a time BEFORE STRINGS when he was perfectly repulsive and deserved everything that a certain Big Man in the Sky could throw at him!

The boy's name was Calloway. He was a lazy boy whose nickname was Calloway Can't, because when anyone ever asked him to do something helpful he always said, 'Can't.'

'Right,' snapped his father, chucking the dustpan and brush to the floor. 'If you won't clear up your own biscuit crumbs, go and do your homework instead.'

'Can't.' Calloway was lying on the sofa picking his nose.

'What do you mean, *can't*? *Can't* implies it's physically impossible. So what's happening here? You can't do your homework because you haven't brought your homework home, you've lost your pencils or your brain has gone on holiday without leaving you a note?'

'Just can't.'

'You mean you don't want to?'

'No. Can't.'

'OK!' Calloway's father controlled his temper and tried to make his next suggestion sound like fun. 'Let's go and help your mother lay the table.' He even put in a little jump as he walked to the door to make the prospect seem exciting!

'Can't.'

'Oh, how convenient.' Now he was angry. 'Go and tidy your room!'

'Can't.'

'What *can* you do then?' he exploded.

Calloway picked his nose again. This time with more success. 'Nothing,' he said as he licked his finger clean. His father was defeated and slumped into the nearest armchair. Calloway's activity of choice was always nothing, because Calloway had the get-up-and-go of slow-growing mould.

He didn't like being told what to do. He said it was because he was nagged twice as much as any other child, because his parents were teachers who ordered him around at school as well as at home. But this was just an excuse to cover his laziness.

'Lay the table,' said his mother, later.

'Can't,' said Calloway. He was slouched over the kitchen table counting the hairs on his forearm while his parents rushed around him preparing supper.

'There's no such word as *can't*,' his father said through gritted teeth.

'So what word did I just use then?' cheeked Calloway, causing his mother to spin round from the stove with a whiplash of sarcasm.

'Praise be!' she cried. 'A whole sentence without the word *can't*!'

'If all you ever say is *can't do this, can't do that*,' persisted his father, imitating Calloway's bored nasal drone, 'you'll never do anything! You'll just tie your life up in knots until it fizzles out in a splutter of non-achievement!'

'I'll never do anything *you* want me to do,' Calloway spat back.

'Oh, Daddy, did you hear that?' mocked Calloway's mother. '*Two* sentences without the word *can't*. This is so exciting, Calloway. You're having your first conversation. Do carry on.'

'Can't.'

'Don't cheek your mother or I'll put you in detention,' snarled his father, forgetting he wasn't at school.

'Can't.' At times like these, when Calloway was being particularly lazy and stubborn, Calloway's father liked to introduce a small bribe to jolly his son along.

'If you lay the table we'll take you with us to see *Pinocchio*!' he said. Calloway gasped. That was below the belt! He really wanted to see that show. But if it meant doing something he didn't want to do. No. Nothing was worth that compromise.

'Can't.'

'You mean, won't!'

'I'm not your puppet!' Calloway yelled. 'I don't

jiggle around just because you're pulling my strings!' Calloway's defiance only seemed to excite the mischief-maker in his mother.

'Oooh!' she taunted, chubbing her son's cheeks with her fingers. '*Three* sentences, Calloway! Has Christmas come early?'

What Calloway didn't know was that someone with their head in the clouds was listening to his every word; someone who turned bad children into toys, whittling their limbs into tethered lumps of wood!

* * *

Later that night, while Calloway snored like a beached whale, there was an urgent tapping on his bedroom window.

'Let me in!' whispered a faint, whistling voice outside. 'Wake up! Your life is in danger!' Calloway woke with a start and sat bolt upright. His racing heart thumped in his ears as he searched the darkness for a face. 'Hurry, Calloway. Laziness strengthens his hand. Let me in!' Calloway turned slowly towards the window, unsure of what he would see. 'Save yourself. Say *can't* no more,' said a wooden-toothed smile. Framed in the window, hanging from the sky by strings and staring back at Calloway through matt black eyes, was a clown puppet.

Bizarrely, Calloway's reaction was fury. Instead of showing fear he leaped out of bed, threw open the window and grabbed the puppet by the throat.

'Can't you tell how funny I think this is,' he yelled, bursting into his parents' bedroom, and thrusting the puppet under their noses.

'What's going on?' mumbled his father, waking from a deep sleep.

'Take that out of my face!' yawned his mother.

'I'm not an idiot,' shouted Calloway. 'I know what you did.' He mimicked his father's voice. '*I say, Mummy, before we go to sleep, shall we play a joke on Calloway? Because he's our puppet and has to do whatever we tell him to do, let's put a* real *puppet outside his bedroom window and pretend it can speak! Ha ha! Can't stop laughing.*'

'It's not ours.'

'Of course it's yours. Who else would it tell me to stop saying *can't*?'

'We've been asleep.'

'Well, somebody climbed onto the roof, hung it outside my window and whispered

73

in a spooky voice!' Calloway's father looked like he'd just seen a ghost.

'The Puppet Master!' he gasped.

'The Puppet Master!' mocked Calloway. 'Is that really the best you can come up with? You can't scare me!' But his father was serious and showed his son two red scars on the back of his hands. 'He taught *me* a lesson when I was a boy. He only left me alone when I stopped saying *can't*.'

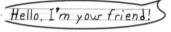

'You expect me to believe that?'

'It's true. Promise me you'll stop saying it too!'

'Can't,' said Calloway flippantly.

'Don't test him, Calloway. The Puppet Master takes you at your word. When you say *can't* he makes sure you mean it. He'll tie you up in knots so you'll never be free to do what *you* want again.'

But Calloway still resisted. 'I can't see him,' he said, 'so it's not true.'

'Have you ever seen the Puppet Master in a Punch and Judy show?' asked his father. 'No. But that doesn't mean he's not there, does it?'

Hello, I'm your friend!

Not a sausage!

Just like Gilbert, whom we can also hear but not see. Although I KNOW that Gilbert's NOT there, because I ate him!

Calloway ran back into his bedroom and hurled the puppet out of the window. He heard a rustle and a thump as it landed in a flower bed. Then he threw himself onto his bed and forced himself back to sleep. Behind his back, however, as the stars flittered between the clouds, a small muddy figure rose up outside the window. Half-lit by the blue moon it swivelled its wooden eyes, fixed its stare on the hunched figure in the bed, opened its pink felt mouth and grinned.

See what I mean about a puppet opening its mouth without a hand up its bottom . . . SCARY!

* * *

The next morning, Calloway was tired and grumpy when he left for school. It was drizzling so he wore

his coat. He ran to the bus shelter and stood half in and half out of the rain, testing the depth of a puddle with the heel of his shoe. As he suspected, it was deep enough to soak the bottom of his trousers. When the bus arrived Calloway joined the queue to board, but as he did so something moved inside his coat. It thrashed in the bottom of a deep pocket like a trapped cat. He grabbed the lump through the lining and exerted pressure to calm it down. A few seconds later, after the bus had departed, Calloway found himself alone.

'You!' he stammered, as his eyes met the blinkless stare of the wooden marionette from the night before. 'But how . . . I threw you away.' The puppet showed no sign of life and lay limply in Calloway's hands. 'What do you want?' At this, its eyes came alive. It raised its head and its limbs became taut.

'We are brothers,' it said, in that same whistling voice. Not having seen the puppet speak before, Calloway was so shocked that he dropped it like a hot potato. But it didn't fall. It bounced in mid air and returned to float in front of Calloway's face. He tried to run, but the marionette blocked his path.

'Puppets can't speak!' screamed the boy, swiping it

out of the way with his arm. 'When did you learn?'

'When I was a boy,' it said, swinging back on its strings. 'Like you!'

The great thing about boys made of wood, of course, is that unlike real boys they have their uses; they BURN which means you can boil water on them to make a nice cup of tea.

Just then, Calloway felt a hand brush his shoulder. The hairs on the back of his neck stood on end as he spun around, but there was nobody there. A hand brushed his other shoulder, then jabbed his wrist and prodded his knee.

'Who is it? Who's there?' Someone was toying with him! He went to look over the other shoulder, but this time turning round was harder, as if a giant hand had gripped his shoulders. His brain was telling him to flee to the safety of school, but his body was out of control. This unseen hand was forcing him to turn back the other way. Towards the theatre!

A noise made him look up. His throat gurgled with horror. His legs buckled, but like the

Bzzzzzzzzzzzzzzzzzzzzzzz

I know how to spell HORROR, thank you, Purnellopy

marionette, he did not fall. Soaring into the clouds above his head were eleven straight strings. Each was attached to Calloway's body: two to the ankles, two to the knees, two to the elbows, two to the hands, two to the shoulders, and one to his lower jaw running up through the top of his head. They twitched like the filaments of a spider's web and Calloway's feet jerked forward.

The strings yanked him into the air, tugged him through the branches of trees and swung him round a lamp post like a rag doll. They dragged him across the bonnets of cars in a car park, and through the soft fruit on a market trader's stall.

'Oy!' came the shout from the greengrocer. 'Stop that!'

'Can't!' bawled Calloway. 'It's not me!'

'Never say *can't*!' warned the marionette, having blagged a free ride in Calloway's coat. 'You'll only encourage him.'

'Who?' wailed the boy, as he bounced off a traffic light. 'Encourage *who*?'

'Look up,' hissed the marionette. 'See who's pulling your strings!'

Peering out of the clouds like a tortoise hanging

from its shell, was a Goliath of a man – the size of God, only less infinite and more human. A huge bearded face with a velvet beret on top and an old man's hands clutching a wooden cross attached to eleven strings; the strings with which he now controlled Calloway's every move. It was the Puppet Master in all his terrifying glory!

'I am your Master now!' he roared. 'You can't say *can't* to me!'

Which was absolutely true, because the Puppet Master controlled the string that opened and closed Calloway's *mouth*!

Then the Puppet Master tugged Calloway's strings all the way to the theatre and left him hanging on the stage, so that when the curtain went up for the first night of *Pinocchio*, the audience got more than they'd paid for. As the lights lit up the Toymaker's set, Calloway's parents screamed.

Their son's dream had come true. He had made it to the theatre, but instead of *watching* the show, he was in it. And instead of taking the audience's cheers and applause, he took their screams and running feet. The show closed before the interval. Calloway's parents were the only people who came back for the second half, when they sat in the front row and listened to their son whisper in endless repetition;

'I can now. I can. I can now. I can. I'll never say *can't* again.'

* * *

It took two days to rescue the human marionette from the stage, because every time the fire brigade tried to cut through the tangle of strings Calloway cried out in pain. When they brought in a mobile X-ray machine they discovered that the strings were fused to his bones. Eventually, they made a hole in the roof and craned him out over the dome. The Stage Door was locked and bolted and Calloway was driven home in an open-topped lorry with all strings still attached.

* * *

That was two years ago. Life at home now is very different. Laziness is a thing of the past. At six o'clock every morning the Puppet Master tugs Calloway awake and gives him his daily chores.

'You can help your mother with the washing up today, and after that you can make the beds and sweep the kitchen floor! Tug tug! Up you get!' The house has never looked so spick and span, because now Calloway *can* and always *does*!

But that's not all. Last month my housekeeper was consumed by cockroaches, so I had a quiet word with the Puppet Master and Calloway DOES down here now as well. He's what you might call a SCULLERY PUPPET, but I would call My Little Treasure. He's a whiz with the duster and nothing is ever too much trouble. The other day I said; 'Can you scrape the loos with your fingernails and suck that spider's web out the chimney, Calloway?' And you know what he replied?

'Of course I can, Mr Night-flight Porter. Shall I climb into the oven while I'm about it and lick off all the grease?'

Lovely boy! So helpful!

I've just had a text message:

wot s u ccret?

Is it an alien from another universe trying to get in touch or is it some smartie-pants brat who wants to know my secret (what I stupidly told you about earlier) and has forgotten that I've now got his mobile phone number?

oy brat scred? u shd b

Bzzzzzzzzzzzzzzzzzzzzzzzzzzzzzzzzzzzzzzzz!

That's Purnellopy again. No. it is spelled right. PURNELLOPY. That's the thing about names: you can spell them any way you like. My name. for example. The Night-flight Porter. is spelled. GERALD GOOSEBERRY LUCY FORTESCUE DEATHMASK BEELZEBUB BLACKANGEL. or NICK for short.

THIS IS A TRUE STORY: When I was a teeny-tiny baby I lived on a cloud and was given a little toy bat by my godmother. Not a cricket bat, a shrunken-faced furry thing with sharp teeth. It ran on batteries and ate flies. Anyway, she told me it was for good luck, but she was having a laugh, because two days later I dropped it out of my cot and instead of stopping when it hit the cloud it carried on falling . . . for THREE days! It plummeted through skies, seas, rocks and volcanic lava flows until eventually it landed down here in this hothell. That's how I came to be here in the earth's core. I crawled after it and couldn't get back home. Well, I was only a couple of weeks old and I hadn't been taught how to use a bus yet.

the Night-flight Porter

THINGS YOU CAN DO TO MAKE TOYS MORE DEADLY

Another good idea from The Deadly Toy - Makers'Club
Number 100

Play Catch with a Porcupine

It's funny how some toys like a Stradivari violin, a Van Gogh paint brush or a million—pound cheque can bring GOOD luck, whereas other toys like chainsaws, flame-throwers and full-size, practical balsa wood glider kits can bring BAD luck. Personally, I think we should add 'Any Toy Thrown Out of a Cot' to the 'bad luck' list, because I'm not the only one to have suffered. This next tale, for example, is a tragic tale of poverty, ignorance and multiple deaths at the hands of a baby's rattle. So expect lots of laughs!

Hello, I'm your
friend!

tap tap tap tap tap tap tap tap tap tap tap

Why do boys have sticky fingers?

I CAN NOW. I CAN!

Bzzzzzzzzzzzzzzzzzzzzzzzzzzz

THE DEATH RATTLE

The baby was a girl and still had no name when her father gave her the rattle. It had cost twenty-five pence in the hospital shop and was made out of blue plastic. He pushed it into her tiny hand five minutes after she was born, then went off to get her mother a cup of tea. Five minutes later, just as he was re-entering the ward, the girl dropped the rattle over the bars of her cot. It rolled across the floor and under her father's foot. He slipped and spilled scalding tea over her mother, who leaped up screaming and put *her* foot down on the rattle as well. In lurching forward, she grabbed onto the lapels of the girl's father's jacket and knocked him back towards an open window which sucked them both in and spat them both out on the other side, where they plunged to their deaths in the gutter below like a pair of wingless pigeons. At eleven minutes old the girl was an orphan. The death rattle had changed her life for ever.

> If that's not bad luck I'm a pot-bellied pig's underpants!

The girl's grandparents, Sid and Doris Underblanket, drove up from Southend and said they'd look after her on two conditions. The first was that she should never be allowed to have another toy, because they didn't trust her not to drop it out of her cot and kill them too. The second was that they should be allowed to name her.

And so it was that the baby girl was named Purnellopy Underblanket. Her grandparents had never been good at learning on account of never having turned up for school, preferring the education afforded to them by parks and bus shelters and the wisdom passed on by the birds. What they knew they had learned from life, and the biggest lesson they had taken in that time was that people respected a bit of class. If you had a name

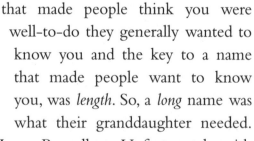

that made people think you were well-to-do they generally wanted to know you and the key to a name that made people want to know you, was *length*. So, a *long* name was what their granddaughter needed. Hence Purnellopy. Unfortunately, with no education, the longer the word the harder it was to spell.

'Purnellopy can be anything she wants now,' said Doris. 'King, Queen, Lady in Weightlifting. We've done her proud, Mr Underblanket.'

'As proud as a kipper,' said her husband, a telephone engineer by trade. 'Here, my dove, what do you think to my new Business Card?' It had a picture of a telephone on it and the words *Mr Syd Underblanket – Lektronik Voyce Wave and Speetch Transpoortashun Consultent.*'

'It's beautiful,' said his wife. 'I never knew you were so important.' He wasn't.

* * *

As Purnellopy grew up and learned to speak she noticed that she was treated differently to other children her age. She never had anything to play with.

'Can't I have a toy pub like what all my other friends have got?' she asked.

Sid explained that she was different to other children, because most children didn't kill their parents in the first eleven minutes of their lives.

'It weren't her fault,' protested Doris. 'It was the rattle's.' And to prove how much it was the rattle's

fault Doris took it out of its
shoebox, spat on it and threw it
out of the window. 'That,' she said,
as the rattle landed in the mud, 'is what I
think of toys!'

CRE

Little did MRS STUPID realise that the
act of throwing the rattle away was what had
started the family's bad luck in the hospital, and
now she'd gone and thrown it away AGAIN!

'So what *can* I have to play with?' asked
her tearful granddaughter.

ZJA

'*This!*' said her grandfather proudly.
'You may not know it yet, angel-poops, but this
here object is the best type of toy that there is.'

MR

'A spelling book!' groaned the
disappointed girl.

NOP

'It's a heducational toy!' he said. 'Mrs
Underblanket and I want you to have all the
advantages what we never did. It learns you stuff
that will make you brainy and get you a good job!'
It was a large red notebook tied up with ribbon.

FB

'What you do,' explained her grandmother, 'is
write any new word that you come across into this
book until you've written down every single
word in the English language.'

KTS

'It will be your own private dictionary,' beamed

old Mr Underblanket. 'Oh Mrs Underblanket, don't it make you well up!'

'Don't it just,' she sobbed as tears rolled down her cheeks.

'Learning,' he sighed. 'That's our gift to you, Purnellopy! You learn all of those words in that book and you'll be so clever that you'll be able to do whatever you want. The world will be your flipping ostrich.'

* * *

Well, the world could indeed have been Purnellopy's flipping ostrich had it not been for one thing. It wasn't that Purnellopy was resistant to learning, she wasn't; and it wasn't that she was upset at only being given a 'heducational' toy instead of an ordinary one, that wasn't it either; it was the fact that her spelling teachers were her grandparents, and her grandparents couldn't spell.

When she came across the word automobile for example, she asked her grandfather how to spell it.

'O,' he said, 'R, au-to, TOE, mo, MOE, bile, BEALE. Easy. ORTOEMOEBEALE.' So that's what she wrote down and that's what she learned.

And that's what happened with every word she put in her spelling book.

See Shaw
Elliefant
Tellervisjun
Derveener Muckall
Skool
Fast Food Restrorn
Bloo
Plassderseen
Detenshun
Toylet

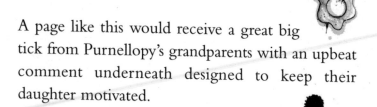

A page like this would receive a great big tick from Purnellopy's grandparents with an upbeat comment underneath designed to keep their daughter motivated.

Well dun, Purnellopy. We will maik a newclear signtist owt of yoo yet!

The trouble was that Purnellopy received so many ticks in her spelling book that when she finally went to school and was taught how to spell properly she thought her English teacher was having her on.

'How did you become a teacher when you don't know how to spell?'

'I *do* know how to spell,' said Miss Dobbs. 'It's *you* who needs to learn.'

But Purnellopy thought she knew everything and argued with the teacher when Miss Dobbs tried to correct her mistakes.

'No!' Purnellopy whined. 'I haven't got it wrong. China is spelled TCHINA. It's *you* who doesn't know your aunt from your elbow. It's in my spelling book at home!'

'I'm sorry but there is no T in China,' protested Miss Dobbs.

'So what have we been drinking all these years then?' squawked Purnellopy. 'Of course there's tea in tchina. Blimey! Don't be such an ignorant!'

Sometimes Purnellopy would become so angry with her teacher for saying that she didn't know how to spell, that they would have a stand-up row in the classroom and Purnellopy would be excluded from school for her bad use of bad language. When she got home she would tell her grandparents which words Miss Dobbs had said she'd spelled wrong and they would shout.

'Flipping teachers! Never knew nothing and still don't!'

'How can you spell words wrong when you've got your own Spelling Book!' said her grandfather. 'Spell me *brilliant*.'

'BRYLYANT,' said Purnellopy. Her grandparents beamed and clapped their hands.

'That's you, that is,' said Mr Underblanket, kissing her hand as she curtseyed. 'You're brilliant!' Which is exactly what Purnellopy thought she was, when, later that night, she laid her head on her pillow and went happily to sleep.

She doesn't do that anymore.

* * *

Purnellopy's grandparents thought they were being kind to their granddaughter by telling her that she was the best, but all they were doing was turning her into an obstinate child who thought she could do no wrong. That night, outside her bedroom window, driving rain buried the death rattle deeper into the mud and Purnellopy's luck slipped slowly from bad to worse!

The following day, Miss Dobbs announced that there was to be a Spelling Bee after lunch. There was a county-wide competition, and each school had to send its best speller to take part. Naturally, when Miss Dobbs first told Purnellopy's class, Purnellopy thought that she was a shoo-in.

'Well, I am the best speller in the school,' she said to her friends.

'No, you're not,' said Anthony Foley, who regularly got ten out of ten for spelling. 'All of us can spell better than you.'

'How dare you!' screamed Purnellopy, slapping Anthony's face as if he'd just called her a rude name. 'I'm the only one with a Spelling Book.'

'In which everything's spelled wrong,' he hissed as he fought back the tears.

'Well, we'll see, won't we?' she crowed. 'We'll see who's best this afternoon!'

It wasn't Purnellopy. She spelled *excite* EGGSIGHT; *trouble* TRUBELL; and *castanets* with a K and a Z. Anthony Foley won hands down and high fives up and was chosen to represent the school in the county final. Purnellopy was beside herself with fury.

'I was robbed!' she screamed, then added witheringly, 'That's robbed with two Ds in case you didn't know, Anthony.'

'Purnellopy, calm down,' said Miss Dobbs. 'You are just going to have to accept the fact that you aren't the best speller in the school.'

'Oh, I see what you're saying,' sneered the slighted girl. 'You're saying that my Spelling Book is *not* a heducational toy after all, and because I can't spell, I can't possibly have a good job, is that it?'

'Absolutely not!' protested Miss Dobbs. Spittle bubbled from the corners of Purnellopy's mouth as she stamped her foot. 'So you want me to have a *bad* job, like scraping poo out of dog bins or eating rats on cable TV!'

'I don't know where you get these ideas from.'

'No, don't tell me!' shrieked Purnellopy. 'Ideas . . . it can be spelled two ways. A boy spells it IDEERS, but a girl spells it IDEARS.'

'Go home,' snapped Miss Dobbs, catching Purnellopy's fist as she swung it towards her. 'And only come back when you can behave like a sensible human being!'

Think how *nice* Purnellopy *might* have been if she hadn't thrown that rattle out of her cot. Still, let's look on the bright side. if she hadn't become so vile I would never have had the pleasure of making her life ~~a misery~~ sheer joy!

Sid and Doris Underblanket were furious when they heard what Miss Dobbs had said about their granddaughter. They would have gone into school and given the teacher a piece of their minds, but they didn't have a piece to spare. Instead they lightened Purnellopy's mood by telling her an extraordinary story that they'd once heard about a Spelling Bee.

'I'd never heard of the term until Miss Dobbs used it this morning,' said Purnellopy.

'It comes from America,' said Sid. 'Just after World War One there was a famous bee in Louisville, Kentucky that was very good at spelling.'

'Really?' goggled his granddaughter.

'Stripe me down if I'm lying,' he said.

'You mean there are bees in the world that can spell?'

'They invented it,' said Mrs Underblanket.

* * *

That night a twisted plan formed in Purnellopy's head to get back at Anthony Foley. All she had to do was challenge him to a return Spelling Bee and with certain devious things in place she would humiliate his pants off! All she needed was ONE BEE! One that could spell, obviously.

She went for a walk in the park with a jam jar hidden behind her back and pretended to smell the flowers. Had anyone spotted her manic eyes, however, they would have known immediately that she was hunting for bees. As they landed on the petals to suck up the nectar, she scooped them into her jar and slammed on the lid before they could get out. By the time she got home she had captured twenty-four bees.

Up in her bedroom she inspected each bee individually. Holding its wings together with a pair of eyebrow tweezers she put her ear next to the bee's little mouth and said, 'How do you spell—' she thought she'd start with an easy one '—*bee?*' she said.

The bee did not reply. Not a cough, not even a clearing of its throat. It just hung there dumbly. 'Well, you're useless,' said Purnellopy, squashing the poor insect with the fat end of a hammer that she had brought up to her bedroom for that express purpose.

> 'To bee or not to bee; that is the question . . .'

Six hammer blows later there was still no word from the bees. That was when she thought that maybe they talked with their wings! She gripped the next bee around its neck and was rewarded with a furious buzzing noise that sounded horribly like, 'I'll sting you I will! I'll sting you when you're asleep. See if I don't!'

That one went the way of the hammer too, as did the next four, but the twelfth bee out of the jar was a winner. It was huge, about three times the size of all the others and spent most of its time asleep. When this bee droned next to Purnellopy's ear she swore it was speaking to her. Its gentle buzz seemed to undulate like the rhythm of human speech and when she asked it to spell *revenge*, her favourite word of the moment, she fancied that it did!

> I bet even a bee couldn't spell *discombobulating*.

* * *

Convinced that this fat lazy bee was the answer to a bad-speller's prayers, Purnellopy completed her evil plan by sending a letter to Miss Dobbs, in which she begged her teacher's forgiveness and asked if she might come back into class. She told her that she was no longer confrontational and to prove it, would happily take part in another Spelling Bee so that Miss Dobbs could see how much she had changed.

It worked.

On the following Monday morning, Purnellopy inserted the fat bee into her right ear and went to school. She had seen a detective film that weekend in which a female detective had been instrumental what to say to the bank robber by the voice of her Chief Constable talking to her through a tiny speaker in her ear. This was where she had got the bee-insertion idea from. Her plan, in case you hadn't guessed, was to go head to head with Anthony Foley and beat him at spelling using the bee's superior knowledge. If she made Anthony cry while she was doing it, so much the better!

The class waited expectantly while Miss Dobbs

asked Anthony to spell *flange*. He was spot on.

'Your turn, Purnellopy.' The teacher shuffled her cards and looked directly into the girl's eyes while the bee buzzed to let Purnellopy know that it was still there. 'Spell *terrapin*,' said the teacher.

'Oh, that's easy,' said Purnellopy, stalling for time. The bee was buzzing away inside her head, but it was hard to make out what it was saying. 'I think it's T . . .' she said. 'Yes? TERRORP . . .' She hesitated; then appeared to talk to thin air when she snapped, 'Well, make up your mind! Is it an I or a Y?'

'Is there someone I can't see in this room?' asked Miss Dobbs.

'Not at all,' said Purnellopy, hurriedly covering her gaffe. This bee was hopeless! She would have to spell the word herself. 'So that's TERRORP . . . Y.'

'Wrong,' said Miss Dobbs. 'First blood to Anthony.' And because she'd promised to behave, Purnellopy had to sit there with a smile fixed on her face while she lost.

It took a lot of smiling before she was allowed to go home. She lost 25-0.

* * *

Back at home she hurled herself into her bedroom and poured scorn on the bee in her ear.

'You're useless and stupid and it's all so unfair!' she wailed, throwing her Spelling Book against the wall. Then she stood up and bashed the left side of her head with the heel of her hand to make the bee fall out of her right ear. She had the hammer ready to teach it a lesson. But the bee must have sensed the danger, because it refused to drop out. She tried to pull it out with tweezers, but it simply snuggled down deeper and nestled next to her ear drum, where it purred like a cat as it drifted off to sleep.

* * *

That night, Purnellopy cried herself to sleep.

With six zs.

She had a dream in which she extracted the bee from her ear with a miniature ice-cream scoop. She laid it on the table in front of her and hit it repeatedly with a rolling pin until it burst open like a red grape. As she did so, a loud buzzing started in her ears. At first, she thought it was another bee, but

CREZJA MRNOP FBA KYS

then realised that it was
the sound of people from
all over the word chattering,
laughing and shouting her name.

'I never liked that big bee,' they cried. 'Three cheers for Purnellopy!' The whole world was talking about her. They were calling her the greatest speller who ever lived, just as her grandparents had always told her she was. Her spelling book was taken away to be exhibited in the Museum of Mankind, as the finest living example of man's mastery of words. The people were cheering now. The buzzing in her ear had grown louder and louder and louder still . . . when she woke up!

She was in her own bed, only the buzzing in her ears hadn't gone away, and it wasn't people talking about her spelling either. It was bees buzzing. While she had been sleeping a swarm of bees had swooped through her window searching for their queen, around which instinct drove them to build their new nest. Unfortunately for Purnellopy, an eagle-eyed drone had spotted the queen inside Purnellopy's ear. There was nothing she could have done to stop them. Bee by bee, the swarm squeezed itself down her tubes and made itself at home in her head!

In the morning, when Purnellopy's grandparents came in to wake her, they were greeted by they most extraordinary sight they had ever seen.

'Well, knock me down with the weather!' exclaimed Mr Underblanket, while his wife burst into tears. Their beloved granddaughter, for whom they'd had entertained such high hopes, had been turned into a human hive. The bees went in through her ears, came out through her nose and when she cleared her throat she coughed up honey!

I'm delighted to inform you that Purnellopy's bad luck didn't stop at a headful of bees. I've got her down here now in The Darkness, teaching English to all my guests. Well I wouldn't want them leaving here being able to spell, would I? She scares their pants off as well, which is always a bonus! All that buzzing in her ear has driven her MAD. If she's not shouting at the walls telling the noise to stop, or eating flowers, or jumping out the window claiming she can fly, she's clinging to the ceiling upside down puking honey over their heads!

She thinks she's a bee. If you don't believe me, read this poem, which she wrote while she was pollinating my favourite black tulip.

A SPELLING BEE

A is for AKORN wot falls off a tree

B is for BIZZY wot I like to bee.

C is for COAM wear I put all my huny

D is for DRINGKING the DUE wen it's suny.

E is for ERIK (a grate frend of mine)

And F is for FLOWUR wot stinks quite sublime.

G is for GRARSE wot the cows luv to chew,

H is for HUNY or HIGHVE, up to you!

I is for INSEKT, a singular breed,

And J is for JAMM wot is scrummy with swede.

K, now then K is for KWEEN BEE or KWEST,

Whereas L is for LEEF wear I land for a rest.

M is for MEDOE witch everywun nose

Is wear I get NEKTAR from flowurs wot grows.

O is for ORINGE whoes blossom is sweet

And P is for POLUN wot sticks to my feet.

Q is for QUONTAM, that's Physiks to you,

But R is an R'D one – I haven't a clue!

S is for SWORM wot us do in a bunch

With STINGUS a-plunjin to pack us a punch.

T's TALLIE-HOE, hour scream wen we's flying

And U is for UNDERCARRIDGE

Wot we drop to stop dying.

V is for VAAN with a grill wot is slatted

W's the WINDSCRENE on witch I get splatted.

X is for XMASS and perishing toes

Wen YUST about YEVERYFING'S covered in snows.

And Z is for ZZZZZZ, a regular sound

Wot I make in the hej wen I'm buzzing around.

Purnellopy Underblanket

Form Bee

103

> tap tap tap tap tap tap tap tap tap tap tap tap tap tap
> tap tap tap tap tap tap tap tap tap tap tap tap tap tap

You'll have to type up, Eric. I can't hear a word you're writing.

By the way, the death rattle was picked up out of Purnellopy's garden by a school teacher. So if you see a blue baby's rattle in your toy box at school why don't you change your luck and drop it on the floor . . . GO ON! See what happens. I DARE YOU!

> tap tap tap tap tap tap tap tap tap tap tap tap

That's better, Eric. I can hear that. Now there's just the tiny problem of not having a clue what you're saying. Is it something to do with a dripping tap?

Eric's a weird one. Some people are born human, some achieve humanity, and some, like Eric, have humanity thrust upon them when they'd much rather live their lives as gun-totting aliens, boy racers, elastic superheroes and even sonic hedgehogs. I'm talking of course about Games Geeks, Computer Nerds, Techno-Twits, that odd bunch of night owls who avoid the company of human beings and, given the choice, would move INTO their PCs and bivouac down with a cocoa!

EBOY

His name was Eric, or Bloodthirst the Battleaxe to give him his full Game-Name. At school they called him Toad on account of his big bulbous eyes which he'd got from spending all day in the dark, and his wide flat fingertips that came from bashing buttons on a keyboard. The only time he ever came out of his sunless bedroom was to go to school. Eric lived on his computer. He shopped on it. He chatted on it. He listened to music on it. He kept secrets on it. He played games on it, and, of course, he slept by the light of its screen saver! The only thing he couldn't do on his computer was open a door and live inside it. Because that's what he wanted to do, live in a cyberworld where games were all that mattered. On countless occasions he'd tried to find a way in through the back of his computer with a screwdriver and torch, but he'd never managed it.

Until the day of the argument.

* * *

It started like any other day with Eric tearing himself away from his computer to go to school, and coming home at three thirty in his usual mad way. The most traumatic seconds in Eric's day were those precious in-between seconds when he *wasn't* at school and *wasn't* playing on his computer; in other words, that frustrating No-Play Zone known as 'travelling to and from school.' Eric hated those wasted minutes when he could have been logged on, which was why he'd developed his eccentric route home. It was the quickest way back to his computer.

EXTRACT HACKED FROM ERIC'S SECRET DIGITAL DIARY

Timecheck – 15.30: Bell rang. Had rucksack packed and ready to go by 14.12, so was first out of classroom door. *Timecheck — 15.30 + 09 seconds:* Jumped on skateboard, which earlier I had cleverly tethered with slipknot round back of bike sheds. *Timecheck — 15.30 + 10 seconds:* Speed-wheeled out of playground. *Timecheck — 15.30 + 12 seconds:* Nearly had accident as I pulled out onto pavement. Missed dog's tail by

inches. Ran over its head. *Timecheck — 15.30 + 18 seconds:* Hit low wall around raised flowerbed. Catapulted into air. Performed double forward somersault and landed on back of dray horse pulling cart of beer that passes same spot every day. *Timecheck — 15.30 + 21 seconds:* Kicked horse on. It broke its harness and we galloped off towards canal. *Timecheck — 15.30 + 29 seconds:* Stood on horse's back as it plunged into water, and jumped up to catch hook dangling off chain dangling off crane. *Timecheck — 15.30 + 32 seconds:* Used momentum to swing across canal. At top of swing let go and flew. Landed on Church Steeple. Checked time. *Timecheck — 15.30 + 33 seconds:* Had made up 3 seconds thanks to excellent galloping. Made mental memo to take carrots in tomorrow to thank horse - if they'd got it out of canal by then. *Timecheck — 15.30 + 35 seconds:* Shinned up steeple to thin bit at top, which couldn't take my weight and bent over till it touched roof of next door building - my house! *Timecheck — 15.30 + 39 seconds:* Ran across 'steeple' bridge and up to roof ridge where rope attached to chimney. *Timecheck — 15.30 + 45 seconds:* Holding rope, swung out into sky like Spiderman and sailed back through open bedroom window. *Timecheck — 15.30 + 49 seconds:* Let go of rope and landed in office chair. *Timecheck — 15.30 + 51 seconds:* Chair wheels slid across polished wooden floor and dropped into four specially drilled holes in front of desk. *Timecheck — 15.30 + 53 seconds:* Locked into position in front of computer. *Timecheck — 15.30 + 54 seconds:* Switched on computer. Come on! Come on! *Timecheck — 15.30 + 59 seconds:* At last, the world's slowest computer booted up! *Timecheck — 15.31:* Game on!

One minute after leaving school, Eric was sitting in front of his computer shooting virtual monsters. Little wonder then that his parents should have been so concerned about their son's health and mental well-being. What made this day different from all the others, however, was that this was the day they decided to do something about it.

THINGS YOU CAN DO TO MAKE TOYS MORE DEADLY

Another good idea from
The Deadly Toy-Makers' Club
Number 7,002

Cross breed a Tamagotchi with a Rotweiller

Normally, Eric's bedroom was a No-Go Zone. His parents were not allowed through the door unless they could produce identification cards verified by the latest biometric technology. Today they simply ignored the retinal scan, barged in and started shouting.

'Back from school less than two minutes and already you're glued to that chair!' bellowed his dad.

'Look at you! Sitting there, goggled-up to your screen.'

'Anyone would think you were *made* by a computer,' sobbed his mum. 'You spend more time in its company than you do with your own mother!'

Hearing raised voices, Caspar the black cat poked his head around the door. Nobody shouted at him to go away so he slunk through the gap. Normally he was banned from Eric's bedroom in case he ate Eric's goldfish Megabyte but this time, because of the argument, nobody paid him the slightest bit of attention. Nobody except the goldfish, that is!

'I just wish you'd *do* something with your life!' cried his mother.

'I do lots of things,' replied Eric, keeping his eyes fixed on the screen. 'I fight alien invaders. I crash cars. I blow up planets.'

'Yes, but it only uses your eyes and fingers. It's hardly exercise.'

'And my brain! If I didn't use my brain my eyes and fingers wouldn't work.'

If he didn't use his brain he'd be a footballer!

'Very clever,' snapped his dad. 'But while you're busy being cheeky that computer will be the death of you.'

Behind Eric's head a black shadow leapt onto the table where the goldfish lived. Megabyte tried to attract its master's attention by plunging up and down in its water and blowing bubbles as loudly as it could, but a paw soon put a stop to that, followed by a set of sharp claws and a vice-like jaw full of teeth.

* * *

Meanwhile, oblivious to the massacre behind them and despairing of ever changing their son, Eric's

parents left the room. As she closed the door, Eric's mum had the last word.

'You're so stubborn, Eric, it's like talking to a fridge magnet!' Eric was fed up with his parents interfering in his life and telling him what he *could* and *couldn't* do. He turned back to his computer and typed a short e-mail message. **GET ME OUT OF HERE**, he stabbed with his stubby fingers. **I WANT TO LIVE IN CYBERSPACE!**

Now, what made this message different to any other he'd ever written, was Caspar the cat, or rather what Caspar the cat had just done. As Eric pressed SEND, he caught sight of the empty goldfish bowl and shot out of his chair with a shriek of 'Megabyte!' He lunged across his computer table to grab the guilty cat, but Caspar slipped through his fingers and screeched out of the door, leaving Eric to complete his lunge through thin air. With no cat to grab, his fat fingers knocked the bowl, tipping water all over his desk and into his keyboard. A barrage of sparks spat out of the back of the monitor followed by a thin plume of smoke. Then the e-mail message disappeared and the screen went blank.

Eric was beside himself with fury. He had broken

his beloved computer. How careless could he be?! He felt like a blind man who by mistake, had cooked his guide dog in a microwave by mistake. Talk about a self-inflicted wound. He slumped onto his bed and flung his head into his hands.

Beep.

He twisted over his shoulder to look.

Beep.

He couldn't believe his eyes. There were four words on the screen. **PHANTOM** and **POSTMAN, FIND** and **ME**.

After Googling the words, Eric discovered that www.phantompostman.com was a website. Instructions on the home page ordered Eric to scan in a full length picture of himself, attach it to an e-mail and press SEND. He followed the instructions but as he pressed SEND, he felt a strange tugging sensation in his lower stomach, as if somebody was trying to pull a plug out of his bottom. He doubled over as the pain increased, only to yelp and spring upright as the plug popped out. With a loud farting noise, Eric took off towards the ceiling and fizzed around the room like a deflating balloon before careering at breakneck speed towards the glass screen. As he cried out, the letters of the word he was screaming typed themselves out of his mouth.

'Helllllppppp!!!' In a long straight line the letters pierced the air like the blade of a broadsword, before his body ingested itself, turned inside out and evaporated in a puff of smoke.

* * *

When he re-materialised Eric's landing was unforgiving. With a sickening crunch he fell onto a hot brick path and grazed the palms of his hands on some gravel.

'You have just been e-mailed,' announced an automated American voice. 'Welcome to the Firewall.' The sky was raining leaves of hot ash.

Eric rubbed one out of his eye. 'Firewall?'

'Everyone walks through fire. No firewall; no entry to cyberspace.' Even as the computer talked the bricks burst into flames.

'Stop,' shouted Eric. 'Or I'll burn to death!' The automated voice made a noise like a small outboard motor, which Eric realised was a pre-programmed laugh.

'Stand still or I will delete you!' it said. Against his

better judgement, Eric did as he was told, but could not help himself from crying out when the flames consumed him.

'Aaaaa . . .' He stopped in mid-scream. 'Actually, that's quite pleasant!' he said. The flames were warm, but completely painless. Their heat made him light-headed and before he knew it, he had lifted off like a feather and floated through a tear in the clouds.

* * *

Eric popped out of a letterbox into a cold, blue room, where an orange uniform was waiting to interrogate him.

'Good morning, Eric,' it said in a gently-soothing female voice. The uniform had no arms, legs or head sticking out, so was basically just a uniform. 'I'm your Cyberspace Assessment Officer. Please stand on here.'

'Am I in cyberspace?' gasped Eric as he stood on the metal plate in the middle of the floor.

'Tch tch tch! You're seven stone overweight.'

'But I only weigh seven stone.'

'Have you been tampered

with since you left your bedroom?'

'Tampered with!?' snorted Eric.

'Could anyone have opened you up while you weren't looking and planted a virus?'

'I think I'd have noticed.'

'Good,' said the uniform. 'We don't like viruses in cyberspace. Still have to have you smaller, though.'

'Smaller?' said the boy. 'I can't get any smaller. My body's *designed* to be this size. Anyway, I thought cyberspace was infinite.'

'No,' she chuckled. 'Barely thicker than a slice of Parma ham. The atmosphere would sustain your body mass for a microsecond, but then you'd explode. So we have to strip you back to bare essentials.'

Eric wasn't sure he liked the sound of that. 'And how are you going to do that?' he asked warily.

'Worm therapy,' she said, shoving a contract on a clipboard under Eric's nose. 'Sign here, please.'

Before Eric could catch his breath a robotic arm shot out of the floor and manacled his right wrist. At same time, a robotic arm burst out of the ceiling, thrust a pen into Eric's fingers and forced him to sign. The uniform snatched away the clipboard, and hung it back on a hook, which immediately retracted into the ceiling. Meanwhile, a trap door had sprung open in the floor revealing a large tank heaving with slimy, grey worms. Instinctively, Eric took a step back, but this move had been predicted. He was met with a shove in the back from a third robotic arm that propelled him forward and pushed him into the pit, where the worms engulfed his head, tickling his tongue and slithering inside his ears.

'No! Agh! Ow! They're biting!' The orange uniform was standing casually to the side of the tank.

'That's because they're Trojan worms,' she explained. 'Unlike earthworms they have teeth. Now don't worry, they won't eat anything you need.'

Having been thoroughly digested, Eric shot out of the chute at the bottom of the tank and plopped into a square Perspex box filled with a clear viscous solution. There was very little of him left: two eyes, his brain and both hands. They swirled around in the liquid like desperate goldfish resisting the suck of a flushing loo. Then another robotic arm sealed a lid onto the box and Eric was watertight.

Screwed to the bottom of the box was a waterproof keyboard. Eric's eyes floated aimlessly above it, their ragged optic nerves trailing like lifeless tentacles of seaweed. Suddenly, there was a blue electrical flash and the optic nerves twitched into life, plugging themselves into the back of the brain. The muscles tightened, the hands lined up over the middle row of letter keys and the fingers went to work!

'What have you done to me?' typed Eric.

'You've got everything you need to live happily-ever-after in cyberspace,' said the uniform. 'An eye to see, a brain to think and fingers to type. Now hold on tight!'

And without a word of warning, Eric was shot through a portal onto a busy superhighway, where thousands of Perspex brain boxes, just like him, were travelling at the same speed, in the same direction - floating in a sky of games.

Underneath Eric were the white road markings of the superhighway, above and in front of him, lining the black horizon, were thousands of virtual images: a rally car, a hospital, some big cats, a laser gun, a waterfall, a troll, a bi-plane, a dinosaur, and several different types of zombie. Bloodthirst the Battleaxe could choose to play with anything he liked simply by typing in its name. Every game ever invented was literally at his fingertips!

'Laser and zombies!' he typed. Instantly a laser gun materialised outside his box. Using the keyboard to direct its fire he mowed down the advancing zombies, splattering their green blood and brains over the dark void in front of him.

'Yeeehah!' he wrote. Cyberspace was Eric-Heaven!

For all of fifteen seconds.

* * *

Suddenly, there was a loud crunch and Eric's box shuddered to a halt. He had bumped into the back of the box in front. But it wasn't just him. Ahead of him there was a huge pile-up. At the front, a brain box had slammed on its brakes without warning and every brain box behind it had failed to stop.

Eric was checking his eyeballs for bruises when he glanced up and saw something striding across the horizon that made the blood in his brain run cold. It did not take an IT whiz-kid to realise that the computer had been invaded by a virus. Black and jagged, steaming hot with a slash across its ogreish face into which it was stuffing everything it could reach, this fuzzy blob of a creature – with its pumping internal organs on view through its transparent carapace – was huge and growing. Every brain box it devoured increased its size. And it was thundering through the sky towards Eric!

'GO HOME! FLOAT FOR YOUR LIFE!'

Eric jumped when these words of warning suddenly appeared projected on the front of his Perspex windscreen. Brain boxes had broken ranks and were flying back over Eric's head to escape the advancing virus. One had stopped to help him.

'I don't know how to!' typed Eric. He was in a panic. He didn't have the first clue how to steer his box.

'Type in POSTMAN!' wrote the retreating box outside.

Eric did as he was told. 'There. Now how do I get my body back?' He looked up, expecting the helpful brain box to still be there, but he was alone. Little wonder. The cold shadow of the brain box–

guzzling virus engulfed the sky. 'Come back!' typed Eric as something knocked on his lid. His frightened eyes swivelled round to see a cheery-faced postman sitting on a bicycle. As he bent down and picked Eric up, his nose was magnified through the Perspex. It looked huge.

'Tch tch tch!' he tutted. 'You obviously didn't read the disclaimer when you signed it.'

'What disclaimer?' wrote Eric.

'The one explaining that when a body has been eaten by Trojan Worms there's no way back.'

'What does that mean?'

But the Phantom Postman had a job to do .. and there was no time for a chat. 'Hold tight!' he cried, pushing down hard on a phantom pedal. 'Posting now!'

As the virus lunged forward to grab Eric's box the postman swerved deftly to one side and cycled directly upwards into the infinite blackness of Cyberspace, which Eric naturally thought was trillions of miles deep, but was in fact an optical illusion. They reached the roof of the sky in a matter of seconds; seconds after that, the postman had parted the black cloth to reveal the red post box behind; seconds after that, Eric's brain box had been posted and Eric was on his way home.

* * *

A mere two minutes after entering his computer, Eric was squitted onto the desk in his bedroom through an unused USB port. The Perspex box had disappeared in transit so he lay there in his various parts, looking like a stranded jellyfish.

Surprisingly, when Eric's mother found her son's eyes, brain, and hands flapping around in his bedroom, she was happy. She scooped up Eric's bits and plopped them into the vacant goldfish bowl, having first filled it with lukewarm water. Then she sprinkled a small amount of fish food onto the surface in case Eric was hungry and smiled. At last she had her son exactly where she wanted him. If she decided that Eric had had enough computer for one day, she didn't have to argue or plead her case, she simply switched it off at the wall, and there was nothing Eric's brain, eyes or fingers could do about it!

I've done a bad bad thing. I'm so PROUD! One night last week, I sneaked into Eric's bedroom and stole his bits. He didn't notice, because I put ice in the goldfish bowl to freeze his brain for the journey. I've got him down here now, living in a virtual bedroom inside MY computer. Because he feels real pain and real fear he thinks he's still at home, but he's not. He's in a game which I've invented called 'Caspar Goes Fishing'. It takes place at night in Eric's bedroom. Eric is floating around in Megabyte's bowl playing on his computer when the door squeaks open and YOU sneak in as Caspar the cat. I've given you extra-long claws for long-range slashing and piercing. Then *your* task, before Eric's mum comes in and shuts the computer down, is to climb onto the lip of the bowl and fish for bits of Eric. You get 20 points for an eyeball, 30 points for a finger (making 300 in all), and 500 points for the brain. How much fun is that! Not for Eric, obviously. I don't think he's too pleased, especially as I play it for THREE hours every night and never stop until I've speared the brain! Still . . . who cares!

THINGS YOU CAN DO TO MAKE TOYS MORE DEADLY

Another good idea from
The Deadly Toy-Makers' Club
Number 323

Infect Barbie and Ken
with Chinese Flu

Before we reach the end of this Visitor's Book and I LOCK you into this hothell for the rest of your life as punishment for being a short-legged brat, there is a sensitive issue that I need to sort out.

I've had a lot of letters from concerned parents who are worried that if their children read this book and never come back, how will they know where they are? What lovely people your parents must be. They really care, don't they? Well, so do I. It's important, if I keep you here against your will that your parents shouldn't worry, otherwise they might send the police round to look for you and that would just be so, like, BORING for me. Imagine answering the door a THOUSAND times a day and thinking up all those LIES to get them to go away . . . what a waste of time when

I could be teaching you the difference between right and wrong. In case you're wondering; pliers are right but a feather duster's wrong, because it shouldn't tickle.

Anyway, to keep the police away from my door I've written a letter for worried parents. Obviously I can't write a different letter to every parent or I'd lose quality torture-time, so I have carefully constructed a catch-all letter which covers everything I might want to say and everything they might want to hear.

THE HOTHELL DARKNESS
LOST PROPERTY OFFICE

DEAR GRIEVING/RELIEVED PARENTS,

MY DEEPEST CONDOLENCES/GREAT NEWS! YOUR LITTLE HORROR(S)/DARLING(S) IS/ARE NEVER COMING HOME/OUT OF YOUR HAIR FOREVER. HE/SHE/THEY IS/ARE MINE NOW/NOT YOUR RESPONSIBILITY ANYMORE AND IS/ARE DOING SOMETHING USEFUL/BEING PUNISHED FOR THE FIRST TIME IN THEIR PRETTY/POINTLESS LITTLE LIVES. FOR EXAMPLE, I AM DRESSING UP YOUR CHILD(REN)/BRAT(S) IN HIS/HER/THEIR SUNDAY BEST/CONCRETE OVERCOAT(S) AND TAKING HIM/HER/THEM TO CHURCH TO SING IN THE CHOIR/BURYING THEM IN THE PILLARS THAT HOLD UP THIS HOTHELL. YOU CAN BE PROUD OF HIS/HER/THEIR CONTRIBUTION TO OUR LITTLE COMMUNITY/BUILDING DOWN HERE. WITHOUT HIM/HER/THEM EVERYTHING WOULD FALL TO WRACK AND RUIN.

HAVE A NICE/MISERABLE DAY/NIGHT/REST OF YOUR LIFE.

SINCERELY YOURS

The Night-night Porter

Now that you're a guest you can help send these letters out. Ask any child and they'll tell you how much fun it is, and they're not saying it just because I've got their toes trapped in a mangle. You'll get to lick the envelopes and stamps till your tongue's as dry as the bottom of a budgie's cage, then I'll stick your head in the loo for thirty seconds till your tongue's re-hydrated and off we'll go again!

Oy! Where are you going?

You can't just walk out, because you're scared of a bit of slave labour.

I've got a Dolls' House to fill!